The Invention of Love

The Invention of Love

stories

Sara Schaff

Published by Split/Lip Press
6710 S. 87th St.
Ralston, NE 68127
www.splitlippress.com

ISBN: 9781952897009

Cover Design: Jayme Cawthern

Cover Art: "Insulation" by Thuy-Van Vu

. . . I felt too that I might take this opportunity to tie up a few loose ends, only of course loose ends can never be properly tied, one is always producing new ones. Time, like the sea, unties all knots. Judgments on people are never final, they emerge from summings up which at once suggest the need of a reconsideration. Human arrangements are nothing but loose ends and hazy reckoning, whatever art may otherwise pretend in order to console us.

— Iris Murdoch, *The Sea, the Sea*

Love doesn't just sit there, like a stone, it has to be made, like bread; remade all the time, made new.

— Ursula K LeGuin, *The Lathe of Heaven*

for Ben

Table of Contents

Affective Memory

The other night, I dreamt about Luke. We were driving to Point Judith to swim, something we'd never done in real life, because we only dated for one winter, my sophomore year of college. In the dream, he rolled down his window so we could smell the sea air, and I shouted with joy because I've lived in the Midwest for over a decade and rarely make it back east. He told me he was happy to see me so happy. I said the same about him. The dream ended without either of us touching.

When I woke up, I felt unsettled. Not because of the dream, but because I couldn't remember Luke's last name. And Luke had been memorable: funny face, beautiful body, more of a jock than I was used to. Most of the guys I went for were soft, neurotic, and indirect. Luke never seemed worried about anything, and he always said what he was thinking. At the end, he took me sledding, just the two of us crammed into one of those cheap plastic discs.

We slipped far and fast, then fell into the snow, laughing. That's when he told me he had met a girl, and that he thought she might be the one. No prelude or apologies. I wasn't in love with Luke, and we'd had enough fun together, so I told him there were no hard feelings as I brushed the snow from my jeans. Then he drove me home.

I recalled all of this as my dream retreated from me, as I got my daughter dressed and made my coffee. And while I drove to work and sat through the first pointless meeting of the day, I tried to remember Luke's last name. It was a pleasant occupation, my private little crossword puzzle. I decided the name probably started with a

"T," that rang a bell. So during my lunch break, I looked for him on Facebook, typing "Luke T…" into the search bar. And just like that, multiple Lukes appeared to choose from, including the one I wanted—I could tell from his glasses—and I clicked right away on his profile: less hair, broader shoulders. More handsome than he'd been when I knew him.

In his photo, he was standing next to a pretty blonde woman with very long teeth. I'd seen her once at Luke's apartment, long after he and I broke up.

Even after we stopped dating, Luke let me borrow his rusty Toyota Tercel to get groceries once a month. It was the only time we talked anymore—when I picked up or dropped off his car. I really had meant it when I told him there were no hard feelings. I wasn't pining away. But in driving to and from the market, listening to the station he had the radio tuned to (classic rock) and seeing the things he left in the console (dimes, chapstick, protein bar wrappers) I developed a pleasing attachment to him.

So when the blonde woman answered his door, I felt freshly wounded. She was tall and willowy, and she smelled beautiful— like expensive perfume. I stood awkwardly in front of her, my body suddenly too big for me and yet not sturdy enough. I told her my name, why I was there. She smiled in a friendly but distant way until Luke appeared, shaved and showered, threading his arm around her waist.

"Your keys." I held them close to my body, so Luke would have to put in some effort.

"You look good," he said. "You doing good?"

That was the last thing I ever heard from him. I bought an old bike with a large basket between the handlebars and got my groceries that way instead.

Staring at Luke's online picture, reacquainting myself with his name and countenance, I felt satisfied in one regard, but not in another. Because other things returned to me, too: what it was like being the person I had been back then.

I was going through a natural-deodorant phase, thankfully even more fleeting than my relationship with Luke. Also, I had decided I was going to live in Berlin one day because I'd heard it was a good place to be an artist. And I wanted to be an artist, though I hadn't landed on what kind. I wrote melancholy fragments in my journal and spent too much of my work-study money at the art-supply store down the hill from my apartment. I also took acting classes and performed in student-written plays in which I inevitably had to cry about something.

That was why I always got cast, actually. Because I could cry on cue. All I had to do was slip into a sad old memory and let it fill my body, then my eyes. Everything felt so close to the surface in those days—fragile, malleable, electric.

As I walked away from Luke's apartment, I wept without shame, and my body seemed to return to its normal size. I looked at my narrow wrists, my unvarnished, bitten nails. Luke and his girlfriend were already receding from the particular pain of this moment. The sun was hot on my face, the ocean was just a short drive away. I felt alone, so alone, and yet the future felt newly open to me, and I took pleasure in that discovery.

The Invention of Love

Saturday night, no plans to go out. I preferred the quiet of my dorm room to any student apartment that smelled like beer. But at ten when I was already in my pajamas, my friend called and told me about a party. He didn't know the people having it, only that everyone was saying it would be the place to be on Spring Weekend and that he needed to borrow some makeup.

Twenty minutes later he showed up at my dorm with another friend—both of them tall and thin and bearded.

While I sat on my bed under the covers, they applied my eye shadow and lipstick, then turned to me for approval. I found their new beauty charming. My friend leaned over the mattress to kiss me lightly on the cheek, then pulled on my hand. His friend tugged at my other hand.

I changed out of my pajamas in front of them, slipping into the clothes in a pile near the hamper. But the boys informed me that my corduroys were not the right look for spring or even for this decade, which was nearing its end, anyway. Instead, they selected a dress from my closet, a summery one with thin straps and little stars scattered across the skirt. It was unsuitable for the cool night, but when I spun around, my friend and his friend clapped in admiration.

We walked down the leafy streets together, holding hands.

When we arrived at the house, we found it silent and dark. The front porch sagged with couches and bikes. We stood outside on the grass littered with red plastic cups and debated whether to knock on the door.

After a while, the porch light turned on, and a woman several years older than us came outside. She wore tight jeans under a sparkly tutu and a sweatshirt with a different college's name on it unzipped over a low-cut tank top. She leaned over the railing and said hello without smiling. I tried not to stare at her enormous breasts, but her cheeks were so mottled with acne I felt embarrassed looking at her face.

"Is this where the party is supposed to be?" my friend's friend asked.

The woman's expression didn't change.

"Two people fell off the roof," she said, finally. "One of them died." She pointed to where it happened—the parking lot between this house and its neighbor. "The kid who lived fell right onto my car. So in a way, I guess I saved him." Her face was still blank. Shock, I supposed. Or maybe that was just her face. Once I had met a man who had a condition that made it impossible for him to smile.

Now she sighed, then zipped up her sweatshirt, which seemed to take a very long time. She stuck her hands in the pockets and went back inside.

My friend and his friend and I walked back to my dorm in silence. By the time we arrived, I was shivering, even though my friend's friend had given me his jacket, which reeked of cigarettes and spearmint gum.

I invited them in, and we asked a girl down the hall to join us because she always kept fancy bourbon in a little flask on her dresser. We sat on the floor together, passing the flask around, imagining what had happened on the roof. Who had died, who had survived. I did not enjoy the bourbon, so I only pretended to drink it, just to look engaged.

"How did a person survive that fall at all?" the girl from down the hall said.

My friend had been gazing at her hungrily since she stepped into the room. She was short and flat-chested and always wore shirts that slipped appealingly off her shoulders. My friend explained that one person's fall had been broken by the roof of a car parked below.

"I wonder what happened to the roof of the car," the girl said. She stared back at my friend, then kissed him. His lipstick was mostly worn off by this point, but when they parted, some of the coral stain seemed to have transferred to her pretty mouth.

Soon, my friend's friend and I were the only ones left in my room. For a while we just stared at the door. Then my friend's friend tugged at the hem of my dress and started lifting it in the air, then letting it fall again, like one of those parachute games little kids play in kindergarten gym glass.

"I think I'm in love with him," he said.

"Who isn't?" I said.

In fact, *I* wasn't, but the strange night was making me feel annoyed and melodramatic.

"So, you want to do something?" he said.

I felt pretty neutral about this boy specifically, but at that moment I wanted to have someone's hands on me, so I climbed right into his lap.

We had sex on the rough carpet. My knees hurt, but I liked the way he touched my hips—reverently, as if holding up a breakable vase. I kept my eyes open so I could admire the lines of his face. His eyes remained closed. He could have been seeing anything, anyone. I had to keep clearing away images of the students falling from the roof, the arc their bodies must have made, the pressure of the car roof pushing up against the weight of the one who survived.

After, I lay awake on the floor, wishing I could talk to my friend until it was light again. I wrapped myself around the body next to me and closed my eyes but did not sleep.

The following Monday, I arrived late to my lithography class, and my classmates' prints were already hung on the wall, ready for critique. My own print was a boring little drawing of a park bench, and two people sitting on it but looking in opposite directions while clouds gathered in the distance. Just three weeks earlier, when I had first sketched it out, then drawn the figures in on my limestone with my fat, greasy pencil, I had felt the little thrill of discovering something beautiful and profound about relationships. And when I peeled the first proof from the stone, my body filled with joy and pride; I wanted everyone to see what I had made! Now I tried not to convey embarrassment as I pinned the corners of my print to the porous corkboard.

I took my seat on a metal stool, surrounded by a dozen other bodies on stools, most of them drinking coffee from paper cups. As a general rule, the ones who irritated me were the tea drinkers, with their ostentatious little tea bags dangling from metal travel mugs. You always had to hear about the lengths they went to get their special brands, which were imported by obscure shops in Boston or New York. Inevitably, the tea drinkers felt a lot better now that they no longer drank coffee. I always avoided signing up for printing hours with these people.

Our professor arrived late, her eyes red and watery, her blonde hair frizzy and uncombed. Her eyes were always red—from the printing fumes, I thought, or from the Adderall some students said she took to be able to work in her studio late into the night. But this morning she was clearly upset. She just stood in the doorway and did not enter the circle of stools.

"I have some sad news," she said. "Over the weekend . . ."

It was at that moment I noticed we were missing someone: Elliott, the serious boy with the curly hair and ink-stained fingernails. The only truly talented student in class. His figurative pieces were practically photo-realistic, and his abstract drawings always seemed intentional, not scribbled in a blind emotional frenzy.

I always thought he should have gone to art school, and in fact he mentioned that he'd been accepted at the one right down the hill. But his parents said he had to go to here, because although it wasn't Harvard it was still a name his grandparents would recognize, and they were the ones footing the bill. Now he was surrounded by us—liberal arts interrogators who hid our mediocre drawing skills in pompous dissections of line quality and "intentionality." Some students focused only on the social relevance of every piece—"Sure, you drew her face nicely, but I'm wondering how this promotes ideals of female beauty"—and our professor could barely hide her frustration as she steered the conversation back to the work in front of us.

Presumably, we'd all once found something magic in making art—why else were we taking this class? Yet no one ever described the joy they felt in witnessing something beautiful. All of Elliott's prints were beautiful. It was as simple as that.

And now he was dead.

"He's not dead, thank god," my professor said. Her eyes brimmed over with tears, and we all looked deeply into our hands.

She loved Elliott in the way a teacher loves a student who embodies her deepest ideals, who throws himself into the work and doesn't bother to kiss up to her.

He had survived the fall and was now in stable condition at the city hospital. Rather than follow through with critique as usual, our professor had a university van downstairs in the faculty parking lot, and anyone who wanted was welcome to drive to visit him. She'd bought flowers and everything.

Well, it was awkward: who could say no? It wasn't as if we could pretend we had anything else to do; it was 8:30, and our class met until noon. So downstairs we went, and into the van we piled: nine of us, one by one sharing our favorite Elliott stories: that time he found someone's bag of pot in the drying rack (and threw it away!); the other time when someone found his yoga mat and pillow in the studio—he'd been sleeping there for weeks until our professor suggested he get a little more distance from his work.

And that was pretty much it. We ran out of stories quickly. Elliott was such a loner that none of us could claim a real kinship with him. I had printed with him one evening, when he was still sleeping in the studio, and no one had realized it yet. Though he'd been very helpful with the heavy press, which I had struggled to manage, he had barely said a word to me.

No one in the van had been at the party. Which felt like an opportunity for another story. "I was standing outside," I said, "right where it happened." As if I'd had a brush with fame.

The kids in the van turned to look at me, and for a moment I felt that little thrill of discovery again: this time something a little darker, needier—the desire to invent, to be looked at without being entirely seen.

I described the scene my friend and his friend and I had come upon—a scene that wasn't really a scene at all, for the lack of sirens and party debris and bodies.

One girl, a tea drinker with a cheerful nose ring, held my hand all the way to the hospital. I nodded my head and turned to look out the window, to avoid further conversation.

In my head, I replayed Elliott's fall from the roof, as if I'd been standing on it with him, and my palm began to sweat inside the girl's hand, but she didn't let go.

The scene at the hospital was even more awkward than the interaction in the van. We were told by a nurse we would have to wait in the lobby until we were called in smaller groups into Elliott's room, and we would only have five minutes with him because though he was up for visitors, he was very groggy.

Since our hand-holding session, the tea-drinking girl had sort of glommed on to me, and we were among the final group to be trundled into Elliott's room. She put her arm through mine, and we stood at the edge of the bed in a way that reminded me of hospital scenes in movies, but only the ones where the patient has already died.

Elliott was pretty banged up, but he was very much alive. I'd never seen him smile so much, and with his bandages and bruises, his wide grin made him seem a little dopey. "You guys!" he kept saying, then tearing up, then laughing, then tearing up again. He must have been on some serious pain medication. "I feel pretty terrible," he admitted, "but also somehow . . . freer."

He told me and the tea-drinker to come closer, then had me bend close to his lips so he could whisper in my ear. "I've always loved you, Angie. Since the first day of class."

My heart did a confused little flip flop. Angie wasn't the name of anyone in our class, but Elliott continued to whisper the wrong name into my ear. I didn't correct him. I liked the sound of his voice. And anyway, he'd had quite a fall.

That evening, my friend and I went to the dining hall, stuffed our backpacks full of donuts and bagels leftover from breakfast, then went back to my dorm room and made crappy little pizza-bagels in my toaster, which was contraband, but so far no one had said anything against it.

While we ate on my pull-out loveseat and coffee table, my friend told me he'd heard the kid who died had been visiting from out of town. No one even knew him, but he'd just appeared at the house with a couple of buddies, already smashed.

We observed a moment of silence for this stranger, and when I felt it had been long enough, I said, "I know the person who survived."

My friend stopped chewing his bagel and wiped his mouth with the back of his hand.

I launched into the story about class, my professor's tears, the van ride to the hospital and seeing Elliott hooked up to all these little fluid bags and beeping machines.

I left out the part about him calling me Angie and saying he loved me. I felt a little embarrassed for Elliott and didn't want to seem like I was making fun of him. But as I held in this part of the story, I observed my friend looking at me, waiting for me to wrap things up, to deliver some moral or punchline. I had to admit to myself I kind of hoped Elliott really did love me. But I didn't want to tell my friend; it would sound to him like I just had a crush on Elliott because he'd survived something terrible. That I was some kind of love opportunist.

It didn't really matter what I felt about Elliott though, because my friend brought up his friend before I could even digest this new longing spinning in my gut.

"He said you guys hooked up the other night?"

I shrugged and inspected his face for signs of jealousy but found none, which was a relief. "You know he likes *you*, right?"

My friend laughed. "Like that's ever going to happen. Guy's a total narcissitarian."

This was our name for vegetarians who were evangelical about eliminating cruelty to animals but tended to be pretty big shits to the humans they knew.

I don't know why, but I started to cry. Not for my friend's friend, who I hadn't thought about since the middle of the night when he crept out of my room. The tears felt heavy and real, though, not invented the way they had earlier in the day.

My friend hugged me tightly. "Don't worry, you'll get over him."

"I was never under him," I said, trying for a laugh.

"If it's any consolation, he had nothing but admiration for your tits."

"Wonderful," I said. "Exactly what I needed to hear."

It turned out Elliott was more than a little banged up. He failed some cognitive tests in the hospital, and his parents had him withdrawn from school for the semester. Our professor informed our class of this development the following week, and we all hung our heads, then got back to critique as usual.

But there was nothing usual about it. Without Elliott's beautiful work to look at, the conversation became unbearable. Our professor strained to rein in the criticism directed at whatever prints were on the wall.

Since the previous week, I'd made some adjustments to my relationship scene: one of the figures was holding flowers now. I'd ground down the original drawing on my stone, then traced the old shapes in using the marks remaining on the surface. Even I could admit the flowers barely made the piece remotely better, but what I did like were the way the old drawing's lines appeared faintly in the background, like ghostly figures haunting the two people in the foreground.

The girl who'd forged some kind of bond with me at the hospital now discussed these same lines with disdain. "They just look messy to me," she said. Everyone else appeared to agree.

I looked to my professor for some sign of dissent, a nod of appreciation for the process itself, if not the product on the wall. But she wasn't even looking at my print or any other. Her eyes were on the door of the classroom, as if at any moment Elliott might walk in and save her from this banality.

Unlocking the door of my room, I found a crudely folded note under it. I felt my heart speed up and my mouth dry out. I thought of Elliott, writing me love letters from the cocoon of his childhood bedroom. But the note was from my friend's friend, in a barely legible scrawl. He'd had a dream about me, the note said. *Stopped by, hoping to make it a reality.*

It was amazing what dumb things supposedly smart people would say to get laid. I dropped the note in the trash and got out my sketchbook.

I didn't have a plan at first, just Elliott in my head—in particular, I was thinking about this one sketch he'd done for a print he had been intending to complete for his final portfolio. I only saw it by mistake, the night we were printing together in the studio, and his sketchbook was open. He stepped out to go the bathroom, and I'd hurriedly flipped through the pages, feeling overwhelmed at my indiscretion as well as the loveliness on each page, the energy of his lines. Then I came upon a quick sketch of a girl on a bus, reading a book, and everything around me stilled. You couldn't see her face really, because she was looking down, but everything about her posture suggested deep contentment—a total immersion in what she was doing.

When Elliott came back from the bathroom, I was still staring at the page, and he didn't seem embarrassed. I didn't apologize. "I love it," I said. And then we got back to work.

It was the happy posture of this rendered girl that I was thinking of as I drew, as the sky outside darkened. I didn't even realize the door of my room had opened, and then suddenly I felt a figure looming over me, and I shuddered. My friend had been reminding me to lock my door, but I never seemed to remember.

I looked up. Just the girl from down the hall, hair pinned back, revealing her lovely neck. She didn't look happy to see me, so I held my sketchbook protectively, as if it were a shield.

Then her face cracked, and she crumpled onto the floor and cried for a minute. She didn't have to say why; I knew my friend was through with her.

After a while, I put my hand on her back, and she looked at me gratefully. Finally, she smiled, and I could tell she was completely fine now, no more pining. For her it was that easy.

"Can I see?" she asked shyly.

As she turned the pages, I felt the pleasant anticipation of the lover who is about to be touched. Most of my sketches were incoherent, some were erased out of embarrassment, but this girl stopped when she came to the pages I'd just been working on, and I looked at my drawings over her shoulder.

"These are so beautiful," she said.

The drawings were simple, and I took pleasure in her admiring their crudeness. She flipped through the whole book, then returned to the recent drawings again, gazing at them for some time in silence. She even ran her hand over the pencil lines, smudging them a little, but this only made me happier.

Something Else

The city buses went almost everywhere, but not when you needed them to, and never directly. I had to take three different buses to the unemployment office downtown, where I waited for two hours and then filled out paperwork for one. On the bus ride home, I realized I was on the number six when I should have been on the number three, but it turned out the three went right past the grocery store on Maple, the one I could never get Fernando to try. In spite of our diminishing savings, he was still a snob about shopping. Coupons reminded him of his father, who preferred his microwave dinners partially frozen.

I had nothing pressing to do, so I decided to explore. After picking up day-old bread without looking at the long list of ingredients, I wandered to the personal care aisle. The fluorescent lighting flickered and hummed, and underneath it I handled bottles of lotion as if in a trance.

Nearby, a young woman was stocking shampoo. She wore a baseball cap backwards over a green bandana. "I like your get-it girl boots," she said. "Right on!"

I had on these high-heeled boots my friend Marjorie gave me while we were still hopeful grad students. Her parents owned a company that specialized in sustainably crafted shoes ("Locally fed leather," was Fernando's joke). These particular boots were kind of show-offy, their gray leather supple, and I felt embarrassed at the sudden attention, but there were no other customers around to notice. Everyone was at work, probably, and the realization surprised me. Since losing my job three weeks earlier, I'd kind of thought everyone else had nothing to do all day too.

I said, "Thanks, I like your shirt," but there was nothing re-markable about it, except how tiny it made her look. The sleeves came down to her tangerine-painted fingertips.

She flicked open a bottle, held it under my nose. "Smells like coconut cake," she said. "You'll feel like it's your birthday every time you wash your hair."

I didn't need shampoo, but I've always liked birthdays and co-conuts. I saw that she had a nametag. "Thank you for the recom-mendation, Gloria."

Leaving the store, swinging my plastic sack, I couldn't wait to get home and take a shower.

Instead of waiting for another bus, I took the long way home, on streets I'd only ever driven on before our car broke down. The streets were riddled with potholes, and Fernando and I had al-ways complained about the mediocrity of the roads, which were in worse condition than the roads in the outskirts of Bogotá, where his grandmother lived. But as I walked, I could see the benefits. Potholes kept the traffic down. This particular street was lined with big oak trees, and my boots crunched through fallen leaves.

My mood did not hold. At home Fernando was sitting with Marjorie and Tim, drinking wine from our three nice glasses, the ones we'd received for our wedding and hadn't broken yet. Marjorie smiled and offered me a slice of brie on a cracker. It was like a little scene from graduate school—bourgeois snacking before 4:00 PM on a Thursday.

My first thought was, I hope it was Marjorie who bought that very fine wine, but I tried to arrange my face correctly.

She received regular checks of support from her parents. I only knew that because I had snooped around her desk while taking care of her cats when she was on vacation in Bali. Usually, Marjorie pretended to be as broke as the rest of us. She never left the house with more than fifteen bucks in her pocket.

Today Marjorie's flawless skin glowed more than usual. She wore a pair of hand-knit gloves without any fingers, and this annoyed me because she'd promised to make me a pair last year around this time. Our house was always cold, but I still needed my fingers for typing, should I decide to start writing again anytime soon.

Fernando said, "We're celebrating!"

"You got that job?" A quiet relief flickered in my chest. Fernando had been waiting to hear about a contract from a former freelance client.

But he shook his head.

Tim raised his glass. "Marjorie sold her novel."

The tips of Tim's ears were the shade of red I knew well as both envy and lust. He was trying to be happy for her, but it was complicated. In grad school, Tim had been in love with Marjorie, and they'd slept together a couple of times, but she'd told him she found the sex more disappointing than his fiction.

"Oh, that's wonderful!" I said. "I didn't even know it was finished."

Marjorie had an amazing ability to keep her work absolutely secret. She didn't need to complain when the writing was going badly, and she didn't need to boast when it was going well. She just did the work, the way the rest of us went to our day jobs when we still had them.

Two bottles of wine in, Tim cleared his throat. "Not to bring down the party, but I have an announcement to make too."

Fernando was busy loading up another cracker, in spite of his lactose intolerance. I could tell something was up aside from Marjorie's continued winning streak—she'd been published in *Best American Short Stories* last year—and that Fernando already knew and was not happy about it. For the past four years, he and Tim had been working together on a screenplay, and the idea was always to get it in the hands of a friend of ours who wrote for a TV show out in LA.

Tim put down his glass. "I'm moving back in with my parents. My father's coming up next week with the truck to help me move."

He meant he was moving back to rural Virginia, in the Blue Ridge Mountains. Next to nothing but pretty hills and a man-made lake. The nearest café was an hour away. The nearest grocery store did not sell a single organic product.

"But I thought you liked your job," Marjorie said.

Tim laughed. "I'm almost forty, and I'm making barely over minimum wage. What's not to like?"

By this point, Fernando was chain-eating slices of cheese.

Marjorie's eyes filled with tears. "Oh, honey." She was especially pretty when she cried, the way her blue eyes glinted like starfish at the bottom of the Caribbean.

"Can I get a ride home?" Tim asked Marjorie.

She put her small, gloved hand on his thigh and sighed. I could see where this was going.

We all gathered around him in a hug as he stood in the hallway putting on his coat.

Marjorie and Tim left the house holding hands, and I couldn't help it; I stood at the window and watched as she leaned him against her car and kissed him.

"I hate how she takes advantage of him like that," I said.

Fernando was cleaning up the crumbs on the coffee table, wiping them into his open palm.

"Believe me, he knows what he's doing."

"Oh?"

He half-smiled. "Kate, he's moving back in with his parents in a week. He's not going to be having sex for a while."

Sometimes I felt so behind! I never thought like that, in terms of what I needed to do *right now*, because tomorrow it wouldn't be available to me. I had taken opportunities not because of what they meant for my future, but what they meant in the moment.

It's how I got and then lost a job at a local digital advertising agency. Because I was talking to some guy at a party who said they were looking for writers, and wasn't I a writer? He was a writer, too, he declared, red cheeks dimpling. I felt flattered. No one had called me a writer for a while.

At the time, I was working in undergraduate financial aid, which I wanted to care about but didn't. So I said yes to this guy, who soon became my boss, the first supervisor I ever had who wore hoodies to the office. When I started the work, we were doing these email marketing campaigns for car companies I could have cared less about, but everyone on my team was so nice to me and fawned over the corniest bits of copy I wrote—*you are what you drive*—and I just ate up all the praise like a sucker.

From moment to moment I told myself, *This is fine, this is paying our overpriced rent, it's even enjoyable sometimes and the coffee in the break room is decent.* In my down time, I would open up a blank document and pretend to myself that I was working on my novel. I never did get past the first chapter.

And then I started actually enjoying coming to work and Beer Sampler Fridays and was promoted quickly and started buying things I'd always eyed from afar (cashmere sweaters, a new laptop, long weekends at B&Bs).

At first it didn't bother me that my boss called himself a writer, but after a while it annoyed me, the way he bragged about creating the tagline for this kind of sweet liquor famous for being served to underage young women at frat parties and talking about our need to "innovate," as if we worked for Google. I started challenging his ideas at team meetings, or correcting his poor grammar during brainstorming sessions. I thought my colleagues would be relieved to have someone call him out as a fraud.

What I couldn't see was that no one cared what our boss called himself. The 9-5 life is an exercise in tolerance and avoidance. If you saw the boss heading your way, humming the latest Beck song, which he had illegally downloaded via some internet site only he knew about, your job was to smile and nod and return to staring at the blank document on your computer, or to pretend you were frantically trying to complete the copy for the email you'd written in three minutes (but billed the client an hour for). Your job was *not* to engage the boss in a discussion about the challenges of song-writing or the rights of artists to get paid for their work.

When we lost one of our biggest clients to some scrappy start-up outside of Chicago, my job disappeared. As my boss delivered the news to me, solemn-faced, "writer to writer," I thought of my mother, who had never worked outside the home and instead spent all of her time encouraging what she called my "creative endeavors"—the easel paintings, the plays, the storybooks bound with yarn. Before, I'd always loved that about her, and how she managed to make me feel secure, even as my father hopped from one odd job to another. But all her efforts seemed almost naïve now, and not especially practical.

After everyone left, Fernando and I binge-watched a new TV series about a couple of hot adjunct professors who moonlight as prostitutes to make ends meet. It was supposed to be funny and dark in the way that all television was now, and everyone we knew was talking about it: how it subverted our ideas about the American Dream, academia, and feminism. Before we'd even seen the first episode, Fernando already hated it. We were watching to prove him right.

I couldn't concentrate on the show. I kept thinking about what Tim and Marjorie were doing and felt a little gross about it.

Tim and I had slept together just once: the first week of grad school, because it was something everyone seemed to be doing, in addition to drinking a lot and meeting for coffee to complain about the short stories in *The New Yorker* (while secretly, desperately wanting our stories to be in *The New Yorker*). Soon after, Fernando and I got together, and Tim began pining away for Marjorie. Sex with Tim was fine, nothing special, but I have never been the type to get naked with someone and then pretend it never happened. In fact, all my old boyfriends, even the lamest ones, remain lined up naked in a little film reel in my mind that often plays in the background of an average day.

I have never told anyone about the film reel. Except Marjorie, who knows all the weird secrets of my mind and still inspires in me the strongest combination of envy and joy.

As we got ready for bed, Fernando wanted to dissect this big event that happens in episode four of the show we'd just watched, but I already couldn't remember which characters were involved. The two adjunct/prostitutes blended together for me, with their similar shade of honey blonde hair and curvy bodies, hugged tightly by both their clothing and the cameras. I let Fernando go on about the frustrating lack of *real* feminist perspectives in Hollywood while I got into the shower and stood under the hot stream, smelling my coconut shampoo. It smelled fine, but not like my birthday.

"Did you see Marjorie's jeans?" I said, interrupting his commentary. "Those things cost about two hundred bucks."

Fernando sighed. "Katie, no one aspires to be a starving artist."

"No, just an honest one."

Fernando was brushing his teeth. I could hear him roll his eyes on the other side of the shower curtain.

I could be very self-righteous. But so could Fernando. We just used to be self-righteous simultaneously, about the same things. Not that I didn't agree with him about the TV show, or feminism, but they weren't my top priority right now.

Later, my hair still wet, I crawled into bed.

Fernando came in soon after.

"Do you want to talk about Tim?"

"No." He put on his eye mask. "I don't know."

Everything had to be completely dark before Fernando could fall asleep, and then he would slumber through the night while I lay awake, listing my failings in a silent, tortuous loop.

"You applying to any jobs tomorrow?" Every morning I checked the openings around town and at the university. Fernando and I shared one account at a listserv for writers, which is where he sometimes went in search of freelance jobs, now that his regulars had dried up.

"You?"

"Every day, Fercho."

"Hey, it's not like I'm not looking."

"Good, because you have expensive tastes in cheese and wine."

It turned out Marjorie wasn't the one who bought the good stuff, after all. When she called with her incredible news, the first thing Fernando had done after inviting her and Tim over was to walk the few blocks to our favorite little market, the upscale one that sells a million different types of crackers.

"It was a special occasion," Fernando said. "You only sell your first novel once."

"I sure hope so. No one deserves that kind of luck twice."

A week went by without a sign from Tim or Marjorie. And then Tim stopped by with his father, on their way out of town. We sat them down with coffee and eggs, and Tim's father, a man in his late 60s who was all face and hands, asked Fernando about this one script he and Tim had finished years ago, right out of grad school,

the one that inspired them to think about a future together as part-
ners. The script had won some contest and then just sat around in
a drawer.

"The one that got away," Tim's dad was calling it. "What was
it about again?"

Tim rolled his eyes. "It was our first one, Dad. Sappy melodra-
ma."

Fernando adored that script. His eyes shone beautifully just
thinking about it. "The one about a heartsick musician who finds
love with the music critic who judges him most harshly."

Tim was making gestures with his head at me, like we needed to talk, so we headed out to the porch and had a cold-weath-
er smoke, which reminded us of being in class together. During
breaks we would smoke and make fun of everyone else's writing.

"Well, how was it?" I said.

"I always hated that apartment," he said. "It felt good to leave
the keys inside, actually."

"I mean how was it with Marjorie?"

His mouth curved around his cigarette. "We didn't get out of
bed much."

"Ugh. Spare the details, please."

"She said she loved me."

I laughed.

Tim frowned. "At the end, she even helped me pack."

I could see the hope in his eyes. I put my hand on his back.

Tim leaned against me, just a little, and his warmth and weight
felt better than anything had in a long time. The little film reel
started playing without me wanting it to, and I had to pull away
to shut it off. I didn't ever want to sleep with him again, it wasn't

that. But here was someone who'd seen me at my worst—I used to weep over every rejection from every tiny little literary journal in existence—and who still liked my company.

"It's strange," I said, "how we all kind of grew up together."

"Grad School: a Coming-of-Age Story."

We smiled.

"Yeah, no one wants to see that movie," I said.

"Don't worry," Tim said, "I'm only writing action-adventure scripts from here on out."

"And I'm only ever going to see those kinds of films."

Obviously I wasn't serious. Tim knew how I hated action movies. I always had to cover my ears during the explosions. I liked that Fernando only ever wanted to make character-driven scripts. He was in it for the love of the craft, and I thought I was too, though I hadn't written anything for over a year.

Tim sighed, and in an almost-whisper said, "The truth is, Katie, that I'm applying to MBA programs. I'm tired of this shit. If I ever have kids, I'd like their father to be making a real living." He put his arm around me and kissed the top of my head. "I haven't told Marjorie. I haven't even told Fernando."

Poor Fernando. His heart was already broken.

Marjorie called me the next day. She brought over a pie and a Tupperware full of cookies. "I've been baking for the past 24 hours," she said. "I don't know what to do with myself."

She looked terrible. Her hair was a wild poof around her head. It made me feel compassionate. The cookies were dry, but I told her they were delicious.

"Let's go for a drive," I suggested. Fernando was still in bed, surfing the internet and possibly looking for jobs. I had applied to three already that morning before finding a huge typo in my CV and screaming at my computer. "Do you mind if I pick up a few things?"

I wanted to buy the conditioner to go with the shampoo. Also, that morning I'd found coupons for fish. We were out of almost everything, including fruits and vegetables.

Marjorie shrugged. "Fine by me." She didn't blink when I told her where I wanted to go. "I used to shop there all the time."

This was news to me.

"You don't remember? That's the year I got frugal. To, you know, wean myself off my parents' largesse."

"But don't you still—"

She started to cry. "I miss him so much, Katie."

I stared at her until I felt satisfied she was serious. "Maybe you guys just need to be together. Go down to Virginia to tell him! You know, rom-com style."

Marjorie smiled a little. After a pause she said, "Do you ever wonder what would have happened if you and Tim—" she stopped.

I laughed. "Just because I slept with him doesn't mean I love him."

Marjorie sighed and patted my leg comfortably. "I hear the Blue Ridge Mountains are beautiful."

Inside the store, she looked around. The color was returning to her cheeks. She'd pulled back her hair in a flattering, loose bun. Against the dull yellow walls, her beauty seemed ethereal. I'd always thought her skin was so good because she could afford the right creams, but now I could admit she just had really good skin. We grabbed plastic baskets and walked around, arms linked like the old days.

Behind the meat and seafood counter, the woman was missing

all of her front teeth. She smiled at me and Marjorie as she handed me my half-pound of a white fish I had never heard of. Definitely not cod. Everything else was too expensive or over-fished. I worried about both.

Later, looking for my conditioner, I caught a glimpse of Gloria. Swimming in her oversized shirt. Fingernails painted icy blue. She must have felt me staring at her, because she turned and gave me this warm and radiant smile. "Hey!" she said. She pointed at my boots. "I like your get-it girl boots!"

I felt myself blushing from the compliment, although I'd already heard it, and then I had this weird inclination to introduce her to Marjorie, as if we were friends. But then another customer asked where he could find laxatives—he'd heard they were having a sale—and Gloria went off with him to another aisle, without another glance in my direction.

In the check-out lane, Marjorie flipped through the celebrity gossip magazines while I gave the cashier my coupon for the fish. He didn't even look up from the register. His skin was so pale it looked almost blue. As I thanked him, he interrupted me to bother the blonde cashier in the next lane about what she'd done over the weekend. "You still look wasted," he said. His gray eyes became pleased little slivers. The girl tried to discretely flip him off from behind her register, but he kept at it. "I bet you partied with Jaime, huh? I know how it is."

As we walked through the automatic doors, Marjorie said, "What a horrible little troll. That poor girl."

"Yeah." We were at her car. I put my bag of groceries into the back seat.

"I don't remember the store being so—depressing. Did you see the wilted lettuce?"

I had. I'd even purchased some and planned to make a salad with it.

As we pulled out of the parking lot, she sighed. "Thank god we don't work there, you know?"

"At least they're gainfully employed."

I tried to sound annoyed—who were we to look down on anyone?—but I totally knew what she meant. I was 35, overeducated, and unemployed. I didn't know what I wanted to do with my life, but at least I knew I didn't want to bag groceries. I didn't want to admit that I felt superior for believing I had a choice.

On the drive back, Marjorie suddenly got morose. "What am I doing with my life? Writing books? It's so self-indulgent."

Something clicked when she said that. I felt a little story-motor start in my chest.

And then out of nowhere she started crying about Tim again. "Did I tell you the sex was pretty great this time?"

I nodded, but I was living in my head already, dreaming up a story. Woman loses job. Woman loses—if not *the* love of her life, then *a* love. Woman finds . . . something else! Something meaningful.

Home again, I raced to my desk and started writing. I didn't stop until dark, and the front door opened. I heard Fernando in the front hall, taking off his shoes.

I could tell he'd been drinking. I didn't even mind, because Fernando is as pleasant drunk as he is sober. I handed him the manuscript I'd just written—all twelve pages. "Could you read it and tell me what you think?"

He took it from me and sat on the couch. I sat next to him with his arm over my shoulder and fell asleep at his side.

When I woke up, I was drooling onto the cushions, and Fernando was frying up some garlic in the kitchen.

He looked up from the stove and smiled. Oh, what a beautiful man I had married. I waited for him to say something. I started to feel nervous.

"What'd you think, Fercho? About the story?"

He stirred the garlic around and added the fish I bought earlier with Marjorie. He spoke slowly and kindly. "I like it, Katie." He paused. "I like the idea."

"But . . . "

"The friendship with the woman who works at the grocery store? That feels a little forced."

I knew he was right. In the heat of writing the draft, I'd felt the energy of the characters, the bond between my alter ego and Gloria, who—in my story—both put me in my place and reassured me at the same time. I thought I was making good literature. Good social commentary, even. But now, with Fernando not even looking at me, I knew I'd been called out.

I'd bought the fish he was dousing with some white wine, but I didn't want to eat it. I'd made many choices. Big, little, well intentioned. They all felt pretty stupid now.

The next morning, I applied to ten jobs I was overqualified for. Then Marjorie called, and we met for coffee.

She looked great. It made me self-conscious about the bags under my eyes, but then I thought of something that made me feel better.

"Do you think you might be pregnant, Marjie? You have that glow."

"God no. I'm just working again."

She proceeded to tell me that our conversation yesterday "unclogged" something for her. "I wrote the first chapter last night."

I was dismayed. I asked about Tim.

"Oh, poor Tim." She held her coffee cup in her hand delicately, as if it were a bird's egg. "I don't think I could ever be with another writer."

"But he's applying to MBA programs."

Marjorie chuckled. "I can't imagine Tim in business, can you? Suit and tie, all managerial?"

Outside, it was snowing—big, fat flakes.

As we put on our coats, I fished in my wallet for a few bucks and put them under my water glass.

Marjorie handed them right back to me. "It's on me, sweetie." She smiled. "I know something will happen for you. I know you'll find the right job."

I was fine with her paying, but I didn't want her encouragement.

"Here," she said. "I almost forgot. I made these for you last night."

The fingerless gloves: Cashmere. Tiny, perfect stitches. I held them for a full minute, running my thumb over the soft blue yarn, hating and loving Marjorie at the same time, wishing some of her confidence on myself. Some of her talent, some of her luck.

We walked outside together. The snow caught in our hair, our lashes. I put on the gloves and held Marjorie's hand.

House Hunting

Diane stood with her brother in their mother's low-ceilinged living room, her feet sweating in unattractive rubber boots. Their instructions had come from the lawyer: sell the house, pay off their mother's debts, and split anything that remained. Before they could sell, they had to clean. Walls brown from cigarette smoke. Bathtub layered in mold. Carpets that coughed out small, reeking clouds as kitty litter crunched underfoot. Before their mother died, Diane had vacuumed every week and bought special carpet cleaner, eager to do something because she would not do everything her mother asked. Now the cats were elsewhere—the Siamese with Toby's girlfriend, the tortoiseshell with a neighbor—but the smell lingered. Faced with the filthy house, Diane felt like she was being punished.

She watched, aghast, as Toby lit a cigarette. "We're not smoking inside, right? That's what we agreed."

He flicked his ash directly onto the carpet. "We're gonna have to rip out the fucking carpet anyway."

Diane opened a heavy curtain to get at the grimy blinds. Even when she and Toby were in middle school, years before the filth took over, they were not allowed to open the curtains. "You want all the neighbors looking in?" their mother would say. "Watching us eat SpaghettiOs?"

Diane opened the front door, stepped onto the small cement stoop, and took in the view, such as it was: golden arches and the faded sign of a used-car dealership. Next door, a leashed Rottweiler cowered against the chain-link fence that separated her mother's dry brown lawn from the neighbor's greener yard. Each house along this street was one in a train of dingy aluminum-sided squares. Across the way, acres of former farmland had been paved over, ready for more sprawl. She and Toby and the neighborhood kids used to play hide-and-seek in the fields.

Back inside, Diane stuck a five-year-old newspaper under the door to keep it from blowing shut. It was cold and gray outside, but it beat the conditions inside. Against one wall of the living room, shelves sagged with the cooking and self-help books their mother had bought when a little downtown bookstore went out of business. The sofa was piled with sheets and towels Diane had never seen, most of them still in plastic or with their tags on. Cereal boxes and PowerBar wrappers covered the floor. Diane knew the living room had never been worthy of a spread in *Better Homes and Gardens*, but once upon a time you could see the carpet, and her mother had kept that carpet sparkling clean.

"Let's get this over with," Toby said. Diane's head ached. It felt like her fault, this mess, and she wanted nothing more than to get away from it for good.

"Yeah," she said, "let's."

I always thought I'd die someplace prettier.

That's what their mother, Patty, used to say, even before she got sick.

Patricia Kerwitz, née Nason, never hid her contempt for the house where she'd raised her kids. She blamed her ex-husband for buying the house without asking her and then never saving enough money to move somewhere better, once the surrounding hills got sold to developers. Patty herself saved every penny she made, first as a secretary, then as a customer service representative for a line of fine china popular in Russia. She worked in a tiny, grim cubicle, which she rarely left during her nine-hour shifts, but up until the day she lost her job, she seemed to enjoy the routine and even made a show of dressing very well for the office in skirts, stockings, and good leather shoes. When the kids were in elementary school, she would drag Diane to Goodwill on Saturdays to spend hours combing through racks of cardigans, in search of the ones with ribbon-backed buttonholes.

She told Diane, "You dress nice, they can hear it on the phone."

Patty said she'd inherited her sense of style from her French *maman*, a claim that had always confused Diane, because Grandma Nason was born and raised in Spokane.

But over the years, Patty had swapped good cardigans for long-sleeved T-shirts, and after she lost her job—no one was buying fine china anymore, not even the Russians—her old style vanished completely. She'd pretty much lived in sweatpants and flip-flops.

In the past two years, her nest egg had dried up. There were the prescriptions, the doctors' visits, and the panicked calls to 911. She still shopped every Saturday, but now she did it from her couch, while watching the home shopping channels. When Diane and Toby first expressed concern, Patty said she was only ordering the blenders and juicers and saucepans she had always wanted to cook their dinners with, but eventually they'd had to cut up her credit cards.

Up until the end, Patty had begged Diane to move back home with her, but Diane had found the idea too depressing. The smell was already so bad. All the beds were piled with stuff. She had argued there wouldn't be room for her and that, at almost thirty, she was too old to live at home. She didn't say that she valued the minimalism of her own studio apartment, even though its only two windows looked out on a parking lot where businessmen parked their Mercedes SUVs during the day and homeless vets slept under cardboard at night.

But now she was thinking, if she'd been more open-minded, she could have pushed back on the encroaching boxes and trash in her mother's house. More importantly, Patty wouldn't have died alone at night, while Diane was out on a stupid dinner date with the aimless copy-machine repair guy some girls at work thought was cute. While her mother had lain in Diane's childhood bed, taking her last breaths, Diane had been listening to that dope complain about the restaurant. According to him, the waitstaff's manners had vastly changed since last time he'd eaten there, and not for the better.

After work at the medical supply warehouse near Tukwila, Diane stopped at the lawyer's office, which was sandwiched between a Starbucks and a pizza joint in a strip mall off the highway. There were so many papers to sign. The lawyer appeared bored and impatient as she searched for a pen under the stacks of manila folders on her desk. Her blazer was pale blue and baggy, with thick and sloping shoulder pads. Her blonde hair was pulled back in a scrunchie, an accidentally retro look that Diane found comforting, even though the woman never smiled.

"We should talk about whether you or your brother might want the house," the lawyer said.

"I thought we were cleaning it to sell it."

"It's just another possibility, according to your mother's will, if one of you is ready to settle down. If the other doesn't mind being bought out."

Diane said, "Oh, no. Neither one of us would be caught dead in that place." The lawyer looked up from her desk and frowned. "Sorry, that came out wrong."

Embarrassed, Diane signed the papers with her own pen and left.

On her way home, she stopped to see Toby on his break at Best Electronics, and they shared an uncomfortable laugh at the lawyer's suggestion. "Wouldn't be caught dead—you got that right," Toby said.

Hearing him repeat it, Diane felt terrible. They were smoking in the parking lot, surrounded by a sea of empty cars. Toby had been working at the store for eight years, but his uniform had never fit right. The red vest was a little snug around the middle. His army-green pants were too short. He looked like an overgrown Christmas elf, but Diane didn't have the heart to tell him. Toby was the one who'd picked up extra shifts for the past year to keep their mother's creditors at bay, to keep her from losing the house, to pay for the emergency room visits. And now his boss was cutting back his hours, and he would have to find a second job.

Toby crinkled his empty cigarette pack and tossed it into a nearby garbage can. "I'm quitting this time, I swear." He pointed at Diane. "You should too. Carrie says we're digging our own graves."

Carrie was a self-righteous whiner, but Toby's blood pressure was down since he'd fallen in love.

"I don't want to quit," Diane said. During the short days of winter, her cigarette breaks were the only reason she saw daylight during the workweek.

In the morning, Diane drove to Ruston and parked her dented Chevy Nova on the hill above Puget Sound. Her father bought the car in '91 and left the family soon after on the cruise ship he cooked for. That was so long ago now—when Diane and Toby were twelve and thirteen, and Patty still wore clip-on earrings and perfume— but Diane could still imagine her father getting off at the port in Cabo San Lucas and setting up a little surf shop, which he'd always talked about doing. How nice it would be, she thought, to just go somewhere and never come back.

She crossed the railroad tracks and turned onto the sidewalk that hugged the shore. Men were fishing off the nearby pier, and the white sails of pretty boats glinted in the distance. Overlooking the Sound and the railroad tracks, modern glass-filled houses dotted the hill. Their tall windows yawned down at her. In one, a person raised a hand to pull down a blind, and the motion looked so graceful and unconcerned with the drudgery of guilt and house-cleaning.

The image stayed with Diane for the rest of her walk—the small white hand pressed against the glass. Diane knew she would never live in a place like that, with a beautiful view. The kind of view her mother daydreamed of aloud while smoking at the kitchen table, the curtains drawn, the house dark and humid.

Patty had loved those TV shows where the optimistic young couples were looking for their ideal house. At the start of every episode, even the repeats, Patty would lecture the house hunters: "Never settle, kiddos! Never compromise!" But after three houses and twenty-two minutes of airtime, the couple never listened to Diane's mother. The house they bought in the end always had something gravely wrong with it, in Patty's opinion.

"If I were younger and prettier and had some disposable income," she would tell Diane, "I'd go on that show myself. I would show America the meaning of the word 'dream house.'"

The clouds were rolling in, heavy with future rain, but Diane just zipped up her windbreaker and kept walking. She glanced again at the houses perched on the cliffside. A little idea was forming in her mind. The idea wasn't entirely rational or even sane. But it was doable. It was something to do.

That evening at her mother's house, she cleaned out closets and dressers. Twenty-three identical JCPenney bras. Eighteen pairs of polyester pants—green, blue, and gray, sizes eight and ten. Her mother had not been a size ten since Diane and Toby were in elementary school and still sharing a bedroom. She folded each pair of pants and admired the monochromatic pile they formed on the edge of her mother's bed.

Obviously, she wasn't going to tell Toby her plan: looking for their mother's dream home, the place she would have loved enough to open the curtains and let people see inside. The house where she would have preferred to die. Diane didn't know what she would do when she found that house. Clearly, she couldn't buy it. But maybe during the search she'd learn how the owners of pretty houses in pretty neighborhoods used color, arranged furniture, and made small spaces appear larger. Maybe in the process of cleaning their mother's house, she and Toby could improve it.

And in the process of house hunting, Diane hoped she might find the remedy for her guilt.

Thirteen leather purses, dozens of pristine panty hose. According to what she and Toby had talked about, Diane was supposed to put all the clothes and accessories in boxes and bags, ready for the yard sale next weekend.

Earlier that day when she had entered Collier & Nickels, several real estate agents looked up from their computer monitors, but she'd followed one man's smile to the far corner of the room. The way he asked her to sit down—solicitous, pleased, welcoming—it was as if he'd been waiting for her arrival. His name was Mick, and Diane had found lying to him easy, even pleasing. "I'm looking for a house with a nice view," she said.

Mick had answered the way she expected. "You've come to the right place then."

Now, standing in the middle of neat piles in her mother's dim room, she claimed some things for herself. A nice wool skirt she found on the top shelf of her mother's closet. A white silk blouse from the '60s. At the back of one dresser drawer, she'd found five pairs of gloves—one of them kid gloves, the rest made of soft white cotton, some edged with lace, some dotted with tiny beads.

During the drive home to her apartment, Diane pulled on a pair of the gloves: ivory colored, beaded at the wrist. They were too small. She never realized how slim her mother's fingers had been. Grasping the steering wheel with her partially gloved hands, she wiggled her fingers—classy hands, ladylike, detail-oriented.

Diane closed the cool lid of the toilet seat and sat down. This was her first house tour with Mick, and she had never seen a more beautiful bathroom in person. His-and-her sinks, copper fixtures, white marble floors.

Mick waited for her in the kitchen. Before returning to him, she admired herself in the full-length mirror—her mother's gray pencil skirt and a white blouse, tucked in, top two buttons undone. Her shoes were high heeled, rarely worn toe- pinchers. But her legs looked good. She felt pretty and prosperous, her mother's gloves tucked neatly in her purse.

Mick was dressed casually in crisply pressed khakis and a blue Oxford shirt. From the pictures strewn on his desk back at his Ruston office, Diane knew he liked the outdoors: rock climbing, snowboarding, hiking. He was the kind of guy who would look good on television. But in real life, he appeared strangely square jawed, with super shiny hair.

Standing in the spacious guest room, he grinned and opened his arms as if he were hosting a game show. "All the space you might need. And the new asking price is appealing."

In the home's office, Diane turned her attention to the art: watercolor paintings of seaside towns, wedding photos, and school pictures of kids with slicked-down hair. Her mother's house offered up no photos and no artwork, except for the exuberant mural Diane and Toby had painted in their shared bedroom the week they were home sick with the flu. They were nine and ten and alone most of the day. The mural spanned two walls and included mountain ranges that turned into jungles that turned into ocean waves and impossible solar systems. When Diane moved out after high school, her mother began to paint over it but became tired after the primer coat. You could still see the faint shadows of waves and trees, of fish scales and stars.

"I see the wheels turning," Mick said. "You have good taste, Diane. Very good taste."

She nodded politely. She felt she had earned the flattery.

Later, she stopped by Toby's with a car-full of his trophies and posters and the baseball mitts their father had given him every year for his birthday before disappearing.

"What am I supposed to do with this shit?" Toby asked. "I hate baseball. I haven't listened to Metallica in centuries." He flipped through the TV channels, landing on his favorite loudmouthed news anchor.

"I'm making room for a home office at Mom's place," Diane said. "I brought over some paint samples."

"What for? That's why people go to work." He glanced at Diane's shoes. "You're looking fancy, Princess."

Diane flushed.

"You were on a date! The copy-machine repair guy again?"

"God, no."

"Who then?"

"He's a . . . er . . . he's a real estate agent."

"That's so weird."

Of course he wouldn't believe her. "Look, Tobe—"

"Because I met with a real estate agent, too, Di. And I'm not saying my real estate agent is better than your real estate agent, but I am saying that she is a miracle worker. A pro at staging, and she does magic with lighting. You know: Bam! Horrible shitbox becomes livable hovel."

"We'd be lying."

Toby laughed. "It's a game, Princess. Everyone knows it."

"How about we make it nice for real? Put a little creativity into it, the way we did with that mural?"

Toby laughed. He had no idea how serious she was. "How about we move on with our lives?"

They spent the weekend ripping out the carpet. They kept all the windows in the house open, and there was a breeze, but the stench worsened as they pulled back layers.

"We should be wearing hazmat suits," Toby said.

The process was revolting, but Diane experienced a wave of relief with each piece that came unglued.

While Toby went out to get them lunch, she tackled her old room, which her mother had moved into toward the end of her life because she said the cats liked it better. The room was now filled with unopened boxes of jewelry, dusty photo albums, and VHS movies (*Moonstruck, Sleepless in Seattle*) still wrapped in plastic. Diane set the untouched goods aside for the yard sale.

Under her old bed, the bed where she'd found her mother, she discovered a pile of children's books, their pages yellowed. Diane used to read these books at night in the closet so that her mother wouldn't see the flashlight under the crack in the bedroom door. *Little House on the Prairie, The Boxcar Children.* She knew what Toby would say: *To the curb with it all; Carrie says it's time to start over!* Diane took the books to her car and did not tell Toby she had found them.

Diane said she wanted sunlight and water views for $300,000 or under. Mick showed her a studio apartment in downtown Tacoma with a view of the harbor, paper mill stacks, and container vessels. Artists who couldn't afford Seattle anymore were moving into loft spaces in the building, Mick said. From above, Diane could hear the sound of snare drums thumping. "Musicians, too," he added. "The place is going to be hot."

Standing at the front windows, Diane's heart fluttered. Here she was at last: inside, looking out, bright light on her face. She thought she could get used to it.

Still, there was something missing. Diane didn't know what exactly, but she knew it wasn't perfect. *Too small*, her mother might have said. *Too loud.*

At the kitchen island, she perched on one of the leather barstools. "I don't know," she sighed. "I'm not falling in love."

"But it's a nice open floor plan, right?" Mick pushed up his sleeve, revealing a yellow Livestrong band, and leaned against the kitchen island. "Check out this granite."

She shrugged. "I could get used to propping myself up at my own bar, I guess."

Mick laughed, polite and mechanical. His smile, thin lipped, no teeth. She wished she knew what he thought of her. Had he bought her act? Was he tiring of these fruitless tours? Did he like how she looked in this skirt?

She said she'd like a quieter location, so Mick took her to a small glass house on Salmon Beach. The house was built on stilts and surrounded by trees and water. Touring the living room, Diane recalled a recent dream in which a faceless man in a suit pressed her up against a window in a room exactly like this one, down to the cathedral ceiling and the view of Gig Harbor.

Diane actually wanted her own house, she realized, not just renovation ideas, not just closure. She wanted what everyone else seemed to want, and that understanding left her feeling unsteady. She had no savings to speak of. Her credit was in terrible shape. She was still paying off her student loans from the two years she'd spent in college.

When Mick left Diane in the master suite to look around, she sat at the foot of the snow-white bed and put her head between her knees. In the dream and in the house, people in boats could see inside so easily, every lit room a framed painting of seaside life.

She wanted nice windows, she told Mick later. But they didn't have to be so big.

They painted all the walls white. They eliminated signs of smoke stains and water damage. In what was now the guest room, they covered the remaining shadows of the mural.

They got rid of the furniture during one giant yard sale: two televisions, a bedroom set, a coffee table, a velour sofa, a broken La-Z-Boy recliner, and a set of patio furniture. Diane and Toby sat on the front stoop, watching the traffic and the passersby as they poked through boxes of their father's flannel shirts, a tray of mismatched cutlery, even the bed-wedge pillow and bolsters Diane had bought for her mother with her employee discount.

Toby became merrier as the stuff disappeared. "Bargain basement prices," he said, "the only way to move this shit." He cracked open a beer in celebration.

Whatever they didn't sell today would be carted off by the friendly Goodwill trucks. Then, according to Toby and his real estate agent, they were done, except for installing the new carpet. They'd scrubbed, scoured, bleached, spackled.

Diane knew she should be relieved about their progress, but instead she felt like she was merely covering over her error, not atoning for it.

Their neighbor hung around the fence, watching as the sofa got carted off, then sauntered over to poke through a box of their mother's old leather purses.

Diane balked. She had not meant to sell these. She had put the purses aside with a few stained but still-good handkerchiefs she had found in the living room closet. Toby had taken the box outside before she could stow it in her car.

Looking up from the box, the neighbor pushed aside her curtain of long gray hair and smiled. "When your parents first moved in," she said, "I thought your mother was such a lady. I always wondered where she got her taste from, since it wasn't from money."

She held a small navy clutch to her chest. "The clasps are broken on most of these. How much for the box?"

"Three bucks," Toby said, before Diane could protest.

She watched the neighbor take the purses and tried not to cry. "I'm going for a drive."

Toby didn't answer. He was busy making change for a guy carting away a fifty-cent box of their mother's used lipsticks and perfumes—nothing under ten years old.

Diane thought that maybe she should stop seeing Mick. From the houses he had shown her so far, she wondered whether he really cared what she wanted. But in the two-bedroom bungalow that had already been on the market for nine months, something shifted when he steered her into a walk-in closet filled with silks and neat rows of high heels.

"Don't lie to me, Diane," he said, "isn't this your dream closet?"

In fact, it was pretty dreamy. And Mick's look—still difficult to read—was not actually disinterested. He leaned against the wall near the closet door, blocking her way out. He smiled. But the next second his cell was ringing, and he left the room to take the call.

As she listened to him mutter into the phone from down the hall, she slipped off one of her black flats and slipped her toes into a red stiletto. *This could be me*, Diane thought, looking down at her foot in the shoe. Mick returned just as she was buckling the red strap around her ankle.

"Hey," he said, watching her from the doorway. His mouth was set, the smooth veneer descended. She wanted him to say *Go on, put it on, try them all on, they're yours*. Instead, his steady gaze indicated that she should not touch the merchandise.

His eyes went to the necklace dangling just above the low neckline of her clingy blouse. A faux-ruby heart—her mother's old costume jewelry.

They didn't speak on the drive back to his Ruston office. But Diane couldn't help but feel that Mick had seen something in her she had not wanted to reveal. She followed him to his desk, where he sifted through a binder of listings.

"Got any more for me?" she asked, trying to sound professional, not desperate. "The house of my dreams?"

He spread the pages of homes across his desk and gazed calmly up at Diane. "You tell me," he said. The afternoon sunlight glinted off his professionally whitened teeth.

They were hopelessly unskilled, but they installed the carpet themselves: starchy and blue, wall to wall.

For days, the house smelled of carpet. Cheap carpet, coated in dangerous chemicals, thin rather than plush. But Diane felt too tired to mind. On a Saturday evening, she and Toby ordered pizza and ate it with their backs against a recently painted wall. There were no chairs, no tables, no plates. They held their slices with napkins and drank the soda directly from the liter bottle the delivery guy included as part of the meal deal.

Biting off the last of the cheesy corners of her crust, she lay down on the carpet, thinking of the old carpet when it had been new and her mother had let her and Toby sleep on it, tucked under thin blankets, holding their stuffed bunnies to their chests.

"I'm tired," she said.

"Late nights with the new guy?" Toby smirked.

"He's not really—"

"Come outside for a smoke."

She followed him to the stoop, and he lit her cigarette, then looked away.

"They're showing the house for the next few days," Toby said. "We shouldn't be here."

Diane thought of the "them" that would be walking over the carpet with their dirty shoes, rapping at the walls, looking in the closets, wondering what happened here. "No," she said. "Please, call the real estate agent. Call it off." She couldn't get her cigarette to her mouth, her fingers were shaking.

"We're moving ahead," Toby said. "Carrie thinks this will be healthy for you—"

"Fuck Carrie!" She walked around their little square yard and pointed to a patch of earth in front of the house. "Here I could plant tulips. They'd grow well here, it's the sunny part of the house."

"What are you talking about?"

"It wouldn't be such a bad commute. I mean, maybe tack on an extra twenty, twenty-five minutes."

Toby shuttled Diane back into the house and put his hands on her shoulders. "Talk to me," he said. "I'm worried."

He had nothing to worry about. She deserved to live out her days here. "I want the house," she said, finally. "I'll buy you out."

Appraisal, inspection, disclosure. Diane spit her gum into an old tissue from the floor of her car and breathed deeply. *Down payment, closing costs, adjustable rate mortgage.*

As she entered the office, tugging at the hem of her too-short skirt, Mick smiled, his taut skin glowed, but as he ushered her toward the door, he suddenly frowned. "You sure you want to take a look at this one, Diane? There's no body of water in sight."

She nodded. But Mick was staring at her, his usual glassy surface interrupted by an unsettling skepticism. She felt her courage waver. "I have a good feeling?" she said.

"The heart wants what it wants," Mick said, with curious gravity.

Yesterday, Toby said she was crazy and morbid. "Our mother

basically killed herself in this shithole. But if you want it that bad, it's yours. I'm not taking your money."

Today, Diane wanted Mick's professional opinion. More importantly, she wanted to know what the place would look like to the house hunter she was pretending to be.

Unfortunately, pulling into her mother's narrow gravel driveway, Diane realized that this house hunter was not impressed. "They say a little imagination goes a long way," she offered.

Mick stiffened slightly. "They do say that," he agreed.

Watching him peel open the sticky screen door, Diane felt a kind of unraveling in the pit of her stomach. Mick was bewildering today—real, pervious, and, like her character, a bit of a snob.

As she caught sight of her neighbor waving from her kitchen window, smiling quizzically, Diane ducked her head and followed Mick onto the blue carpet. Crumbs of fresh dirt meandered from the doorway toward the kitchen.

"People should take better care," she said automatically, as if chastising Toby.

Mick made a show of wiping his feet on the welcome mat Diane had bought for such purposes.

"Let's start in the bathroom," he suggested, peering intently at the paper listing in his hand.

They couldn't both fit inside comfortably. "I'll put in a slate floor," she said from next to the toilet. She gazed down at the mold she'd been unable to scrape away from the tub. "A rain shower and claw-foot tub?"

"I'm not sure there's room for a claw-foot. A bigger stall shower. *Maybe.*"

In her old room, he sniffed the air. "Cat pee."

"It's not so bad, is it?" What was he doing, pointing out the negatives rather than seeing the house's potential? It wasn't just confusing, it was starting to piss her off. Without thinking, she ran her hand along the wall, the former mural, trailing her fingers down the bumpy paint job.

"A woman died in this room," Mick blurted. When Diane responded with a gaping stare, he shook his head. "I'm sorry. I thought you should know that the place comes with baggage."

He must have thought she might faint, because he reached for her arm and guided her into the kitchen. The kitchen with its vinyl tiles peeling up in corners. She and Toby had finished their work, but she hadn't even begun to address the room's most serious flaws, the fake wood cabinets or linoleum countertops.

Mick slid close enough that she could hear the ticking of his watch, a tinny heartbeat.

Diane stared at his tanned wrists. His cuff links were impeccable. Everything about him stood in stark contrast to the dark claustrophobia of the house. He smiled, and she felt both afraid and hopeful of what he might charm her into doing.

Looking around the familiar kitchen, Diane tried to imagine it with granite countertops and oak cabinets.

I always thought I'd die someplace prettier.

Well, it *was* prettier, now. Or, okay, if not *prettier*, then at least it wasn't quite the shithole it used to be.

"It could be a good starter home," she said, throwing around her recently acquired vocabulary.

"The important question is, can you see yourself here?"

Mick had led her to the threshold. He was backlit now, his gray silhouette blocking the sun. "Think about it," he said. His voice was softer now, and kind. "There are a lot of fish in the sea."

In a moment, she knew she would cry. He was talking to her like he really cared. The living room looked so empty and newly strange.

She hurried to the guest room, closed the door, locked it, and flipped on the light switch. A dull yellow glow emanated from the bare bulb in the ceiling. Quickly, she shut off the light and looked up at the ceiling where she and Toby had forgotten to remove the constellation of star and planet stickers that once lit up the gloom every night as they went to sleep. The answer to Mick's question? She *could* see herself here, and it didn't feel terrible. It didn't feel like punishment. It felt like relief. Without averting her gaze, she felt around in her purse for her cigarettes and lit one. Inhaling deeply, she felt lighter.

"Diane, is everything all right?"

Mick's voice was moving toward her. She imagined his clean loafers padding over the carpet. "Do I smell smoke?"

He was just outside the door now, and Diane opened it with the cigarette still pinched between her lips.

He smiled when he saw her like that, her arms crossed like she owned the place.

She smiled back. She knew what she wanted. "I'll take it," she said. "I'll take it."

We Are Ready

3

Today they were moving back to the city because their mother never liked it here in the country, near the woods. Inside the house, the boxes were packed for the movers who would arrive in twenty minutes. Their mother watched the three children from her bedroom window, a tall window with old and rippled glass. Nora waved, her mother waved back and let the curtain drop. Soon, Nora thought, that window would belong to a thin and pale woman whose children were already grown. Nora imagined her standing at the upstairs window and staring out at the yard like a ghost.

An untended garden ran along the back of the house. In it only hardy mums and wildflowers seemed to grow. The grass hadn't been cut for weeks, but Nora didn't mind—the wilder, the better.

Nora was seven, the oldest. Then came Elijah, who was four, and the baby, Maria Paula, two. They were playing Pioneers, a game of Nora's invention, which consisted of picking up bits of flowers and leaves and berries and pretending to make a meal of them.

"Elijah, make dinner!"

On his hands and knees under the maple tree, his red hair falling into his eyes, Elijah obeyed and began to dig a pit for the oven.

The baby shoved a handful of grass into her mouth.

"Don't eat it for real," Nora scolded. "How will you survive in the woods, if you don't listen to what I say?"

Elijah stood from his crouching position, the denim of his knees streaked with mud. "I know we're not really going to live in the woods." He looked over his shoulder at the dark trees.

Only Nora played there; the small ones were afraid. She and her best friend Naomi had built dozens of forts along the creek in the woods. In the late summer, when the water was low, they hopped along dry stones to the other side. Today, Nora's mother had said, "Stay in the yard where I can see you. We have to be ready."

Nora was not ready. But their mother had found a good job in the city. She had friends there too, and a sister she adored who had a bathtub in her living room. Nora did not want to live in an apartment whose small windows looked out on other people's windows. Once on the subway, she'd stared as a skinny father fed his fat baby potato chips from the bag. And there was the woman shuffling through the aisle singing "Over the Rainbow" into a tinny microphone. Her shimmering skirt brushed the dirty floor, and there was a real bird's nest pinned to her white head, with blue robin's eggs inside it. "Don't stare," Nora's father had said without looking up from his novel.

"Of course we're going to live in the woods," she told Elijah. "That's where pioneers live, because of all the things to eat, and the trees for shelter, and the animals to keep us company."

Rocking forward, Maria Paula collapsed onto her knees and yawned. It was almost nap time. Their mother had said she could sleep in the car on the drive down, which would take almost five hours.

The pine trees of the forest swayed in the breeze, a bright cardinal flitted from one branch to another, and Nora pointed at him as he disappeared.

"He'll show us the best places to fish and hunt."

The three of them turned to look at the house and wave at their mother, who had appeared again in the window. She tapped a finger on her watch. Elijah hung his head, resigned.

Nora lifted Maria Paula and held onto Elijah's grimy hand. "In the woods," she told him, "I'll carve a beautiful chair from the stump of the oldest tree in the world. When you sit in it, you'll have magical powers."

"I want to make explosions come out of my fingers."

It wasn't what she would choose, but she nodded.

For a second, Nora's toes felt frozen to the earth, like in her nightmares, but then she put one foot in front of the other. Together, the children walked into the woods.

2

The children walked into the woods wearing long dresses that dragged in the dirt.

Next to the creek, they found an old canoe on its side against a rock. Nora thought she'd seen the boat before, but Naomi said that it had appeared overnight.

"Help me turn it over," Naomi said. She put her hand on the mossy prow and pushed her veil out of her eyes. "We'll take it down the river, and the fairies will guide us."

"How many wishes will they give us?" Nora wondered, half-listening. The hem of her mother's wedding dress was already muddy, and she realized she would be in trouble.

"No wishes, dummy. They're not *genies*."

Nora's parents had gotten married twice, in New York and in a small town in Colombia, where her mother was from. She was wearing the dress her mother wore in the Colombia wedding. Now Nora regretted taking it down from the attic, without her mother's permission. She regretted listening to Naomi, who had encouraged Nora to wear the dress. Naomi's dress was dirty too, but her mother wouldn't care. Naomi had an entire closet full of dress-up clothes, and they were all machine washable.

Leaning over to help Naomi with the boat, she noticed the blood on the rocks near the creek bed. And some blood on the leaves around the boat. She lifted the skirt of her dress, as if that would help.

When they turned the canoe over, they saw the rabbit, lying still in a nest of leaves. Nora leaned down to stroke his soft, black fur, and he did not stir. "Poor baby. Someone took a bite out of his ear."

"Help me bury him," Naomi said.

Together, they dug a small grave next to a tree stump. Placing the rabbit's body inside it, they sang a quiet song for him, one with made-up words to the tune of "America the Beautiful." Then they covered him lightly with leaves and twigs and a few lilies of the valley.

Washing her hands in the cold creek, Nora saw that her lace sleeves were now dotted with blood.

She turned at the sound of rustling leaves. The rabbit was moving.

"He's still alive," Naomi said. She stared at the rabbit, his fluttering eyelids, and she looked afraid. "What should we do?"

Nora bent down, pushed aside the leaves, and lifted the rabbit gently into her arms. He reared his head back, thumping his foot against her chest. Her mother would know what to do. She pressed him to the dress and kissed his head. His heart beat wildly next to hers.

1

His heart had beat wildly next to hers. Nora's mother remembers leaning into Daniel, thinking, "This is a crazy idea. He has no money. His Spanish is terrible." But Luisa had said yes because she liked how nice he was to her parents. She liked how sure he acted about things. About her. Six months later, she had moved with him to the United States. First to New York, where her sister lived, and where she actually felt happy. Five years after that, they went upstate for his job at a small college in the middle of nowhere.

This was Luisa's life now: for five minutes, she was locking herself in the basement with the dirty laundry, just so she could have some time alone. Her mother was here for two weeks, looking after the children. Luisa could hear them upstairs, getting the better of their abuela, crashing around the playroom and demanding to go outside. Her mother did not want to go outside, not in this terrible, North American winter. It was only a matter of time before Elijah realized where Luisa was and came to pound on the door to the stairs, begging to be stuffed into his snowsuit.

Luisa took the opportunity to light a cigarette. Her husband was dying of pancreatic cancer. Whenever she pictured the world without him, it looked a little like this: low-ceilinged, smoky, filled with dirty diapers and children's tiny, mismatched socks. Sitting on the dryer felt like practice. Later, she would go to the hospital with the children.

Upstairs, she heard a toppling sound and Nora laughing and Elijah saying, "Stop *doing* that, Nora. Leave me alone." And then the baby crying, and her mother's voice: "Tranquila, tranquila, tranquila."

From her husband's hospital-room window, you could see the tops of the trees, the ice hanging from the branches like crystal chandeliers.

She put out her cigarette on the bottom of her shoe and sprayed a can of lavender air freshener. At least if Daniel had been having an affair with his student, she'd have the right to be mad at him. She was thinking of the blonde one who waitressed at that vegetarian restaurant Daniel liked, the girl who'd kept touching him on the shoulder the night of his birthday dinner. At the end of the meal, she'd said to Luisa, "I just have to tell you how much I've always adored *Romancing the Stone*."

Always. Adored. Luisa had wanted to laugh but instead adopted a serious look, to mirror the girl's: "Frankly, I don't think it's Danny Devito's best film."

She and Daniel had left the restaurant smiling, their arms around each other. Only later did she feel annoyed with him for not saying anything in defense of her—but what was there to defend? It was 1995, and there were only three things Americans thought they knew about her country: *Romancing the Stone*, cocaine, and Pablo Escobar. They had no idea that, at her family's house, the bougainvillea tumbled over the whitewashed walls in the courtyard, where she and her siblings had drunk morning tea made of spearmint from her mother's garden.

Now she heard footsteps and Elijah calling for her. Here they come, she thought, her beautiful and needy children. "Ya voy," she said, climbing the stairs. When she opened the door, the gray light of day surprised her.

Elijah threw his arms around her legs. "We couldn't find you," he said, breathless.

Nora stood apart from everyone, her hand on the pile of winter coats by the door. Her eyes were dark and secretive, and Luisa's chest filled at the sight of the girl's good posture and dirty fingertips. Her long braids were coming apart. Just then, Luisa's mother came in, holding the baby.

"It's time to go," Luisa said. Nora was already putting on her coat.

West Lake

When I was nine months pregnant with Lili, I took the train to Hangzhou to punish my husband. I put myself up in the Sofitel, with the intention of living under soft sheets before I became a single mother. When I stepped into my clean and shining room, I felt a little flash of shame about my privilege, which had allowed me this sudden retreat from my life as I knew it.

And yet I was not ashamed enough to avoid room service the next morning. The young woman who brought me my tray of Western breakfast regarded me with frank surprise and, eyes on my belly, asked me where my husband was. "Beijing," I replied, unfazed. "Working." Which was true enough, but still I searched her round face for signs she understood the subtext. She only nodded and left me to my eggs and toast.

I spent the next two hours in bed, eating tiny bites of food and going over the tormented expression my husband had worn three days earlier when he told me he was in love with a Belgian woman, someone he had met on his frequent business trips to London. I did not know what she looked like or anything about her. When I asked for details, he refused to tell me, saying it wouldn't make me feel any better. This only enraged me more. The fact that I could not even picture her in his arms made the betrayal feel worse, I told him, because in this way he had deprived me of even the pleasurable misery of hating her face.

At some point as I lay in my king-sized bed, tray of food to the side since it wouldn't fit over my stomach, Lili began kicking so hard I almost thought I was going into labor. I knew the only way to soothe her was to move, so I spent the remainder of the afternoon walking around the lake.

Xihu, which I had first walked around with my English husband before he was my husband. Willow trees and temples reflected in the lake's glassy surface. The day was hot but bearable. Tourists and locals strolled with small dogs and children. People were friendly and greeted me with smiles and the occasional cheer. I was very large then, but of the opinion that I walked gracefully. Though emotionally I felt weak and depleted, I had never felt physically stronger, and I wore good shoes—running shoes, though I no longer ran—and didn't care that they looked odd with the black cotton dress I'd packed for the trip.

In spite of all the calculations I kept making and remaking (how long before the pregnancy had the affair started, the extent of my stupidity, etc.) as I walked around the lake, I experienced real moments of joy. It was easy to see why Xihu had inspired generations of poets. Something about the water and the rhythm of my walk made me especially aware of the syllables surrounding me, the tones of my adopted language that I had once found so difficult but now thought very beautiful.

On that first afternoon in Hangzhou, a family from Shandong province approached me and asked to have their picture taken next to me, the lake as shimmering backdrop. Once I had written home self-indulgent letters about my loss of anonymity in China and my discomfort at being found remarkable. The "New Colonialism" was what my husband and I called it—the way white people in China were made to feel special for doing exactly nothing more than walking around.

And now here I was, doing exactly nothing aside from walking around while pregnant and white. Yet this family's brief encircling of me almost made me cry from relief. They each in turn told me I was beautiful and fat, laughed at my Beijing accent, and corrected my pronunciation of their village when I said it.

Because of their kindness and the beauty of the lake, I had my first glimpse of a manageable future without my husband. I believed that I would be fine and that my daughter, destined to be born in Hangzhou, would also be fine. At the very least, her Mandarin would be better than mine, and someday she could make fun of me for that.

I realized it sounded a little unhinged, coming all this way to deliver my child, but I never doubted the decision. I'd been happy in Hangzhou before, with my husband, who had taken me here to convince me to marry him and move to China many years earlier. Now I wasn't sure whether it was the place or he that had worked some magic on me. There was a strange kind of logic to delivering our child here without him.

Mostly though, I didn't want him to see his daughter's face the moment she was born. I certainly didn't want him to see *me*, at my most naked and animal, while probably fantasizing about his Belgian lover's perfect body and perfect comportment, both unblemished by pregnancy or betrayal. Without informing anyone but Xu Yan, my closest friend in Beijing, I had already made arrangements at a hospital here, one that served the expat community in the region. Xu Yan had recommended the facility because of its accomplished staff of midwives from both China and Australia. She knew I'd always found the Australian accent amusing. At that point, I felt entitled to be amused.

For those days I waited for my daughter to be born, I spent all my afternoons walking around the lake. After each turn, I stopped in at a café called Starfish, with a green and white logo that would get any coffee shop back home into serious legal trouble. The coffee was terrible there; it tasted like sweat, but I liked the steaming pots of tea and the tables right next to the water. I always had a book tucked into my small purse, though I never read much of it. Instead I stared out at the glassy surface and watched the little paddleboats gliding across it.

The evening Lili was born, I felt winded and had to sit a long while so I could catch my breath. By this time of day, the crowds were thinning. As I waited for my tea, I put my hand on my stomach and felt Lili rolling around. Through my skin, I rubbed what I thought was her sharp little ankle.

I wondered what my husband was doing, aside from going mad trying to figure out where I'd gone. How earnest and aphoristic he had sounded the last time we were here together—*China is the land of opportunity now. I want to make a life there with you!* It's hard to spot the suspicious clichés when you desperately want to get back to the hotel and take off your clothes.

Now the sun was setting behind the distant hills. Something stirred in my peripheral vision. Potted juniper bushes lined this section of the promenade, and in one of them a rolled-up newspaper stuck out of the soil. It was the newspaper that had stirred, and it did so again, this time a quick and insistent jerk.

That's when I saw a man hunched between that pot and another, his legs dangling over the edge of the stone walkway. He was slight; his feet didn't touch the water, which was high that summer. When he turned his face from the lake, blowing the smoke from his cigarette in a slow exhale, I saw that his skin was lined and dark. Dressed in a dusty suit jacket over black pants, the hems frayed, he sang quietly to himself and tapped his cigarette-free fingers against a bag of woven plastic. The seams of the bag were stretched to capacity. I wondered about the contents, where they'd been packed, how far they had traveled to arrive at this corner of Xihu. The man nodded his head to the rhythm of his quiet song, and as the sun disappeared, he became a silhouette against the lighter water.

The newspaper flopped again, and the man turned to it, mumbling. Dropping his cigarette into the lake, he stood up, then picked up his bag and the paper, which I understood now was a fish, recently caught. He saw me staring and nodded, then stuck the fish into the pocket of his baggy pants and walked away.

~

Though I resented my husband for his desertion, I was actually content to be alone. I had been an only child, and though sometimes a lonely one because of it, I had become accustomed to hours of silence, or hours filled only with the sounds I made: reading aloud to my dolls, inventing songs, snapping twigs in the forest to build myself a log cabin. It had been easy enough to become the wife of a rich man, who was often traveling. I kept myself busy with painting our apartment, inventing new meals to make from the produce at the local covered market, and going to yoga class, where I met Xu Yan the year I moved to Beijing with my husband.

At first, Xu Yan and I joked about our status as tai-tais, wives to wealthy husbands, and we played the parts nicely with our manicured nails and beautifully tailored clothing and trips to the salon to get our hair darkened or lightened or blown out.

But the truth was, Xu Yan was not a real tai-tai at all. Her husband was a professor at the prestigious Bei Da, and though doing well, he certainly wasn't as rich as the Western and Chinese financiers in the capital. Besides, it was actually Xu Yan who was the success story in her family when it came to providing a certain kind of lifestyle. After her son started school, she had worked quietly on her own business, making intricate, looped pearl necklaces and exporting them to North America and gaining such acclaim for her designs that I rarely saw her anymore. Her work had been profiled in what I thought of as our local paper, the China *Daily*, but also in international fashion magazines like *Vogue* and *Elle*.

We still met for coffee and sometimes our weekly yoga class, but Xu Yan was usually in New York or Paris or Toronto, wooing clients and attending fashion shows and getting new ideas for her latest collections.

Before I became pregnant, I confessed to Xu Yan my fear that my husband might be sleeping with someone. I did not say I thought it was probably one of the Chinese women who worked as his assistants. Such affairs were not uncommon in my husband's office, or in our circle of friends. One of my husband's colleagues actually called it an "occupational hazard"—leaving one's Western wife for a younger Chinese woman. He did not seem to see the implicit racism or sexism in coining such a phrase, something my husband pointed out in a taxi ride home from that colleague's apartment one summer night, our first summer in the city. Another aspect of New Colonialism, we decided. And I think we felt both comforted and superior for recognizing bad behavior in our fellow foreigners.

I thought I was aware of my own blind spots. My Mandarin was passable, but I was basically illiterate. And aside from Xu Yan, I had no real Chinese friends. No real foreign ones either. Most expats annoyed me. I told Xu Yan it was because I couldn't stand the flock mentality. In reality, the foreign women who annoyed me the most were the ones who reminded me of myself: privileged sidekicks to their CEO husbands, mildly bored with their free time, quick to complain about the air quality any chance they got.

After I told Xu Yan my fear about my husband's affair, she had pressed a packet of herbs into my hand and told me to make a tea of them every night before bed.

"Then what?" I said. "I magically wake up, and my husband's not cheating on me?"

"No." She didn't smile. "You'll sleep better."

"And then?"

"Then you'll have the energy to go out and get a job."

I did sleep better. I did get a job—as a guidance counselor at a small, international school on the outskirts of the city. I liked it, except for having to sit in traffic to get there and back. A few months into the job, I got pregnant. When I told Xu Yan, she lit up. "Wonderful!" Still smiling, she added, "Don't quit your job."

In the movies when your water breaks, it's this dramatic, definitive moment—like Niagara Falls between your legs. But for me, it was just a gradual dampness, and though I thought it might be getting close to time now, I did not hurry.

Now that the sun had disappeared, Xihu looked dark and mysterious—except for the glimmers of purple and green from the light show just north of me. The show began every afternoon as the sun began its descent: electronically controlled fountains close to shore would expel in time to elevator versions of *Moonlight Sonata* and Vivaldi's *Four Seasons*.

In Beijing, I had a good doctor, a man from Shanghai who had trained in the United States at SUNY Buffalo. He had posters of the Bills in his office, and I teased him about their losing streak, but he didn't mind because neither of us actually cared about American football. He had delivered Xu Yan's son, who was now thirteen, and I think she half-recommended him because he looked like Cui Jian, the Chinese rock star Xu Yan had adored as a teenager.

He advised me that when my water broke, I need not panic and rush to the hospital. I would probably be more comfortable at home, walking around the hutongs of my neighborhood. And so, in my temporary home in Hangzhou, I took one more slow walk around the lake, clockwise the way the pilgrims perambulate around the monasteries in Tibet. Though I am not religious, the lightshow and music and the dark around the lake satisfied in me a need for prayer.

I felt relieved that I was on my way to a flock of women to see my child born into the world. Initially, my husband's betrayal had felt like a betrayal by all men. Yet it was my doctor's words in my head as I walked to my hotel, packed up my belongings into my small suitcase, and carried it down to the lobby. *When she's ready, she'll let you know. When she's ready, you will be too.* My doctor's words, but Xu Yan's voice.

In a matter of hours, I would be holding my child in my hospital room. By then, it would not feel like revenge but an opportunity. My husband, probably huddled with his lover in our chilly aristocratic apartment, had never turned down an opportunity. The life that came after this was hard to imagine, but it didn't matter if I could imagine it or not; the next moment would come, and the one after it. I would call my husband, eventually, and he would be angry.

Let him be angry. It was the least he could do.

Noreen O'Malley at the Sunset Pool

Noreen wasn't about to let a baby keep her from doing what she loved. One week in, mostly healed, she pushed the stroller to the community center pool, the carriage draped in a cloth to keep the sun off Derek Jr.'s delicate skin. Her mother had insisted on the cloth and on sunscreen too, which Noreen did not apply liberally because the baby cried as she rubbed it onto his arms. Since becoming a mother herself, she had been surprised by how much she could love this thing that kept her up at night. Still, she could not stand it when he cried.

She got to the center by 10:00 AM, when the pool opened and before the crowds came, and she claimed the one grassy spot under the one shade tree. She parked the stroller under it, put on its little brakes, kicked off her flip-flops, then stuck her feet in the wading pool. Finally, she felt like herself.

Behind her glasses, she took stock of the situation: just a few old white ladies doing laps in the big pool and a few youngish black mothers and their splashing toddlers by the slide and sprinklers. Noreen's friends and former friends wouldn't even be here for another couple of hours. DJ had been awake since six. Before that he had cried from midnight until three.

Sleep or no sleep, better to be out of the house than inside with the television blaring, Grampa Mick in front of it, eating mini powdered-donuts and talking only when one of the little kids pissed him off, when he threatened to beat them with the paddle he kept next to the bed. (The kids—Noreen's sister's—used to be scared of Grampa Mick, but now they laughed behind their hands, because he could hardly get up off the couch by himself, much less lift a paddle to their asses.)

The baby was still sleeping. Noreen got out of the water and set out her big towel, half in, half out of the shade, then lay down on the sunny half of it, belly up. She wore her old bikini, unembarrassed. Her stomach was still a little poofy and pale, but this felt like a medal for what her body had just accomplished. Cristina had no idea. Bella had no idea. *Teen Mom* did not prepare you for the kind of pain she'd gone through or the euphoria she felt after it was over.

Anway, her tits were huge now. Why hide them?

She closed her eyes. Fell asleep with the sun on her face. Woke up to DJ crying. Underneath the sun cover, his face was crunched and grumpy, his hair matted with sweat. And yet he was beautiful. A beautiful noisy old soggy old brown old peanut-sized man. She changed his diaper, then nursed him with her back against a tree. She didn't care who saw.

Only the old ladies in the pool seemed to notice anyway. One of them called to her as she was hoisting herself out of the pool on spindly little arms. "Congratulations, dear!"

Noreen stretched her lips back in an almost-smile but said nothing.

After drying herself off with a towel and throwing on some sort of loose cover-up, the woman was coming right over, in spite of Noreen's grim look. Noreen was familiar with busybodies like this one, judging her, thinking they knew better. Just like Mrs. Newsom, her chemistry teacher, who had once told Noreen she had a good, curious mind and then been surprised to hear Noreen wasn't considering an abortion.

As if aware of a disturbance, the baby stopped nursing and kicked his legs out, leaving Noreen's boob to hang out in the open, the nipple red and sore.

The woman said, "I'm so sorry to disturb you. I adore babies."

She didn't go away. "You want to hold him or something?"

"Oh, may I?"

Noreen shrugged, handed the baby to the woman, and fixed her bikini top. DJ stopped fussing. "He likes you."

The woman stared into DJ's face. "My daughter just had a son too. Anthony Brett Ellis, after my late husband."

Noreen wanted to say, then why not go coo over him, but instead she asked if the woman would hold DJ while she went to the bathroom.

Noreen stepped into her flip-flops and raced to the toilet. She had the most restful pee. She felt as if when she returned to the pool, there would be no baby there. Not her baby anyway. For the moment she had dropped out of out of the strange cycle she'd entered two weeks before: every day exactly like the last, one big loop of diapers, nursing, sleeping. Time had never felt so slow before, and yet the summer was almost over. Her senior year of high school loomed over her, impossible but necessary but stupid when compared with the responsibilities she had now. Trigonometry? How was that supposed to help her get DJ to his doctor's appointments in Lorain?

Noreen took a little longer than usual to wash her hands, to smooth her hair while standing in front of the full-length mirror by the showers, the one she'd always thought flattered her figure. But look—was her nose a bit wider than before? Well, her face was still smooth, her hair thicker than ever. She had a dollar in her bikini top, and she used it at the concession stand to buy a bag of chips.

The families were trickling in now, and Noreen rushed back to the old woman cradling DJ.

The woman said, "You are very lucky dear. Mixed race children are so beautiful." She paused, smiled at Noreen warily, as if realizing her error. "But I probably shouldn't say—"

"Then why say it?" Noreen asked. She took DJ back without

thanking the woman for watching him. This lady had probably worked at the college! Real proof that reading books didn't make you any smarter.

With the sun cover over DJ's head, Noreen held him to her chest and walked the perimeter slowly, not wanting it to seem like she was waiting for anyone, when of course that was exactly what she was doing.

She made it four times around before she saw Cristina and Bella walk in with bright towels over their shoulders, their stomachs taut and tan. They would see her first, she decided. She strolled on, talking to little DJ, cooing into his warm head, all the way back to her towel. Another family had spread out a blanket next to the stroller, their blanket rudely overlapping Noreen's towel. The toddler was peeking into DJ's stroller.

"I don't see the baby," he said, pushing on the handle.

"He needs to be careful," Noreen told the mother. "That thing's brand new."

She stared hard at the woman, who was fat, her skin covered lightly in freckles. She was busy inflating arm floaties for her daughter, and then her daughter ran across Noreen's towel—once, twice—leaving faint tracks of dirt.

The woman smiled brightly. "He won't hurt it."

Noreen glared. People like this woman were what she didn't like about the public pool. No care for personal space or personal property. Let their kids run wild.

She made herself look around, and she felt better. How pretty the water was! That island-blue she loved, and the smell of chlorine that made her think of all the days here with Cristina and Bella and Brittany when they were still good friends.

Finally, thank god, Cristina and Bella saw her and rushed over, cooing, reaching out their hands for the baby.

"He's so amazing!" Cristina cried.

"All babies are miracles," Bella said, in her dopey way.

But Noreen felt proud and tender and allowed herself to smile from relief because she had missed her friends.

"Keep the cover over his head," she warned them. "I don't want him getting burned."

Bella rocked the baby and Cristina asked about the birth, but Noreen didn't want to talk about that, about the doctor and nurses prodding and poking and talking to her like a child. She didn't want to talk about how after, still bleeding, a doctor who had not introduced himself had sewn her tears up while describing the process to a new resident. The resident, a girl who hardly looked older than Noreen, had held her gaze for just a minute, eyes full of pity.

Right now, all she wanted was the latest gossip.

Instead they told her how Cristina had gotten a job at Target and was starting next week, so no more weekday-pool-lounging after today; her life was terrible.

Bella's, too. Her father was still recovering from falling on the ice that winter while delivering mail in town. "I'm sick of making him dinner and doing his laundry," she said. But she said it while looking at the baby and in a baby voice, so she hardly sounded mad.

Noreen nodded and asked Cristina if she would use her employee discount to buy diapers for DJ, but she was still waiting to hear about what she really wanted to hear about, and Cristina and Bella knew it.

The people were coming now. The sun blazed high, and the pool filled, the bodies like hot little dumplings bobbing in the water. Over in full sun, sprawled out, faces down on the lounge chairs were the girls from their school Noreen rarely talked to: white like her but just a little richer (though not actually rich). Brittany wasn't with her pals today, and Noreen wondered why but was pretty sure she knew.

Cristina said, "I want a turn with him," and started pulling DJ out of Bella's arms.

"You've got to hold his head up!" Noreen snapped, reaching for her baby. Gently, she cradled his wobbly little head. "See? Like that."

"Coño," Cristina said, "aren't you the expert?"

"She kind of is," Bella said. And Noreen felt grateful. Bella was the one always trying to puff her up.

Cristina reached for DJ again but he was fussing, so Noreen asked Bella to change his diaper (Bella had a lot of younger siblings and knew her way around Pampers.) And then she told Cristina to take a walk with her to concessions; she wanted a soda and could she borrow a couple of bucks too?

Standing in line, Cristina finally told her what she was waiting to hear, that Derek Sr. was home from college, asking if the baby was his.

"Good," she said. She tried to sound matter-of-fact, not desperate. She had texted him just once that winter to tell him she was pregnant. When he called her back, she could hear his panic—all that hard work, the loans, the scholarships for books, and now this!—so she said the baby probably wasn't his, he should just go to class and not worry. Still, he had kept calling, kept texting, telling her he cared, but she'd ignored him. She'd been young and naïve then. Now she knew better.

Noreen asked the bored-looking kid behind the counter for a large Pepsi and a hot dog for Bella.

"Well," Cristina said, "is he? Is DJ Derek's baby?"

"Of course, dummy, did you actually look at him?"

Cristina shrugged, unconvinced.

"Do you really think I would have named him Derek if—"

Cristina pinched her. "Shut up, he's here. The fucking kingpin and his queen."

Noreen turned. What she saw wasn't a surprise, exactly: Brittany and James, arms hooked around each other, Brittany's bare hip pressed to James' board shorts. Both their hair shiny and sun streaked.

Noreen snorted, though her gut felt wobbly, her legs less sturdy than the day after the baby was born.

"Hi, Mommy!" Brittany said.

Noreen cringed.

Without letting go of James, Brittany went in for a hug, smelling like coconuts and James's cheap after-shave (which smelled like a dying Christmas tree, Noreen always thought but never told him), and she squeezed Noreen tighter than necessary, so that Noreen could feel James against her too, and the memories of touching him came back to her, the memories of fucking him in the back of his parents' pickup truck until she had started showing, which he had said turned him off even more than her period.

When Brittany broke apart, she looked openly at Noreen's deflated balloon of a stomach, while from behind his sunglasses James tried to make it seem like he wasn't staring at her chest.

Noreen believed this gave her a little license to be mean. Pointing at James' ankle, she sneered. "When'd you get the bracelet off?"

He didn't even flush, the little thug. Instead he smiled, and Brittany smiled, and they kissed each other sloppily for a long time before finally telling them the exact date, which Noreen couldn't fucking believe, was DJ's birthday.

James gazed at Noreen, all smug. "I'm rehabilitated." He was massaging Brittany's hip, still staring at Noreen's chest.

"Gross," Cristina muttered.

Brittany said, "You haven't even posted any pictures of him on Instagram!"

Noreen knew what she meant was, they wanted to see who the father was. Reluctantly, Noreen began leading them back to the shade, where she could hear the baby crying for her again. She picked up the pace, but not so fast that anything would jiggle too much. She knew Brittany and James were both inspecting her, and her body right then felt more like a slab of meat than when that doctor was sewing up her pussy.

Cristina caught up with her, linked arms protectively, and whispered, "They're dumbasses. You don't have to let them touch the baby."

"Wasn't planning to."

Bella grimaced at Brittany and James. Noreen sat down and took the baby, who seemed to know her; his eyes took her in, and he appeared to smile. She held him to her and from within her chest she had this new sensation, a powerful surge—both awesome pride and terrible fear. She would do anything for this kid. This kid would be the end of her.

"Wow, Mommy," Brittany said.

"Stop calling her that," Cristina said. "She's not your mother, dumbass."

Brittany rolled her eyes. "But she is a mother, asshat."

James wasn't paying attention to the conversation. On his face, Noreen saw what she'd been expecting: relief, pure and simple. She wanted to punch him. She'd never tried to claim he was the father, though like an idiot, she had hoped for a long time he was.

At least Brittany wasn't making a big thing about it, though she was probably relieved too. They were just awkwardly hovering, waiting for a reason to be excused.

She gladly began nursing DJ. Brittany looked down in horror,

James in disturbed fascination.

"That's, like, legal?" he said. "Out here in public?"

"I'm feeding my baby. Not breaking into someone's house for the hell of it."

Finally, James blushed. Brittany's eyes got mean.

She said, "But don't you want to cover up?"

Noreen smiled. "Nothing he hasn't seen before." She was looking at James, who turned away.

Brittany face crumpled, and she looked for a moment like Noreen's old friend, the one who got scared of Grampa Mick's loud snoring in the other room the first time she slept over, when they were ten—so scared that she had crawled into Noreen's sleeping bag, and they had giggled face-to-face for the rest of the night.

"Congratulations, Nory," she said.

Then her face changed again, smoothed out. Now she just looked happy. Probably that she wasn't in the same situation. And really it was only her good luck that she wasn't. Noreen knew how James was about condoms, and how Brittany's parents were about not ever allowing her to go to Planned Parenthood again, after they'd caught her trying to get pills there.

Same as Noreen's mom, really. Same as her father, who lived in Michigan and rarely visited or sent money but still told her she should have the baby, because it was a life she had created and should take responsibility for.

Finally, Brittany and James walked away, swaying their hips. James shoved his hand down Brittany's bikini bottoms.

The fat mother with the wild kids was still nearby, reading a book. She looked up. "Don't mean to butt into your business," she said, "but if that guy used to be your boyfriend, good riddance."

Bella chimed in, "Amen he's not the father, either."

Noreen nodded. Still, it was hard to stop wishing for something, just because you knew it was a terrible idea.

"Yeah," she said, "he has a tiny dick, anyway."

Bella and Cristina laughed, and so did the woman, who had a pleasant voice, now that Noreen thought about it.

But it wasn't really true about James's dick. It wasn't tiny, just average sized. At least from what she knew about dicks, which wasn't what she would call expert level, in spite of what everyone said about her.

Noreen would have stayed at the pool longer, but she ran out of diapers, and Cristina and Bella got tired of holding Derek Jr., and she got tired of all the kids from school coming up to her wanting to see the latest bastard on the block, or to ask how much it had hurt to get him out of her. She was getting a little bored anyway, and her back hurt from leaning against the tree.

She pushed the stroller slowly, over the cracked sidewalk, until the sidewalk ran out and she had to walk in the street. Her house wasn't far, but by the time she got there, she could feel her shoulders burning, her back was damp. As she lifted the baby from the stroller, waves of heat rolled off him, onto her, engulfing her, and she just wanted to stay out here for a minute longer and have a good cry. But it was too hot to even bother.

As soon as she opened the door, other waves hit her. First, the television: *Ellen*, which her grandfather adored, even though he said Ellen was going to hell. Next, the semi-cool air from the one AC unit in the house that wasn't broken. Finally, the little ones, her nephew and nieces, running over to her, grabbing for the baby, wanting to hold him because it had been all day without him, and she was happy to give him over.

Her niece Stephie held the baby gently and looked from him to his mother. "His daddy's here," she said, "talking with Nana."

Noreen almost collapsed, the way the relief flooded into her body so fast. She'd assumed she'd be the one tracking Derek down at his mom's. She'd also assumed she'd be able to shower first and put on makeup.

As she silently catalogued the failings in her appearance, Stephie handed DJ to Noreen. Derek was waiting. She carried the baby out back.

The yard was tiny and bordered with a chain link fence to keep out the neighbor's dogs, who liked to dig holes in the dirt and generally terrorize the little kids. All the grass was brown and rough this time of year, the flowers her mother had planted mostly wilted. But her mother liked to be out here all the same. She didn't like going to the pool the way Noreen did, because she couldn't stand the noise. Out here, she could read her magazines after work, nap in her lawn chair, and leave the preparation of dinner up to Noreen or her sister or even Stephie, who was competent at boiling water.

Her mother didn't like to be disturbed, but here she was chatting with Derek, who sat awkwardly on a spindly plastic chair next to her.

Noreen watched him for a beat. He'd dressed up for the visit— new jeans from the stiff look of them, and a button-down shirt that was a little too big.

He was saying, "Yes," to whatever her mother was saying. Noreen could only make out a few words: "needs to finish school." Talking about her, probably, but the same could be said for Derek too. He'd been a great drummer in their high school band, if she was remembering correctly. Or maybe it was the trumpet.

No one noticed Noreen was there until DJ let out a little cry, and then the whole world seemed to turn toward her.

Here was Derek's handsome face again, serious and concerned. He'd been serious at Cristina's New Year's party too, when everyone else was drunk and high and optimistic. So she'd kissed him to make him smile. To make James jealous. Look where that got her. Got them.

Derek stood up and walked toward her and DJ. Her joints were melting. She felt like she was going to fall over so she reached the baby out to her mother.

Her mother stood to hug him and kiss his forehead, then handed him right back. "I'll leave you guys alone."

She looked very old to Noreen then, her gray roots showing, her waist indecipherable from the other curves of her body. Perhaps this was Noreen's destiny, this lumpen body, the cheap and infrequent dye jobs, the only moment of peace a minute in your ugly backyard, the dogs next door howling as if they were never fed.

Quietly, her mother went inside.

"How's college?" Noreen asked.

Derek held out his arms for his son.

"I passed. Barely."

This wasn't exactly what she wanted to hear, but she let DJ go. Derek knew how to hold him, and this was reassuring at least, but then he burrowed into Derek's chest, rooting around. "He needs to eat again," she said. "Sorry." She took the baby back, and with that the two sat down in the chairs, Noreen nursing DJ, Derek not minding.

He began to talk.

"College isn't all it's cracked up to be," he said. His classes were huge, no one noticed when he stopped going to some of them. Instead of returning to campus, he was planning to move home, take some classes at the community college, get a job, help her with little DJ. He said, "We could move in together, if that's easier for you."

Noreen began to cry. It was what she wanted to hear, but hearing it, that relief drained right out of her body. Next to her, Derek seemed to stiffen, but he reached over and put his hand on her back and patted her awkwardly.

They barely knew each other. Everyone in school pretended to be cool, but most of them were racist assholes, even her teachers. There were no jobs. Her mother owned this house, by some miracle, but the house was barely standing.

"I always liked that you got out of here," she said.

Derek was quiet for a long time. And then he sighed. Noreen risked looking at him. He was smiling a little, staring out in front of him. "Me too," he said, finally.

Maybe, like James, he was only waiting to be let off the hook. But probably he could see his future locking into place, just the way she could, and this filled her with sadness and shame.

Thank god her mother came out on the back step then and called them to dinner. "You should stay for dinner, Derek. Stephanie made butter noodles."

"Thank you, Ma'am," Derek said. He was looking at Noreen. His eyes were a beautiful, deep brown.

Noreen thought of James and Brittany kissing in front of her at the Sunset Pool, the chlorine smell in the air, the smell she loved, the sounds of the kids jumping off the diving board and crashing into the water with joy. She thought about how James used to tell her she was beautiful, but that Brittany was hot. How ridiculous it sounded now, the kind of thing that should have made her stop wanting him to be her baby's father but hadn't.

Derek was watching her still. "I'd like to stay," he told her. She put DJ in his arms again, and he smiled.

"Of course you should stay," she said. And she thought that he probably would.

Our Lady of Guazá

After the funeral, Abuela tells Marcela and Valentina to sort through their mother's belongings in the living room, which they do, wordlessly and tensely, each putting aside trinkets until they spy something both of them want: a pair of jeans their mother liked to wear out dancing.

"I remember seeing her in them," Marcela says. "I don't know when that was."

"Too small for you," Valentina says. "Perfect for me. Besides, you don't dance in the United States. Remember Tia Mercedes' Independence Day party in Miami?—all her fat gringo husband's fat relatives, sitting around in plastic chairs like at a meeting, drunk and boring."

Marcela can only stare, affronted and helpless. Honestly, she does not miss her mother, but she would rather not be condescended to by her younger half-sister. And, inexplicably, she desperately wants these jeans with the swirls of glitter on the back pockets.

Valentina slings the jeans over her shoulder and puts aside other objects: a purse, a silver tube of lipstick, plastic hair clips.

Marcela sits on the couch. "They won't fit you either," she says. "Our mother was tiny."

"I'll show you tiny," Valentina says. She strips down to her cotton underwear and tube socks, then pulls on their mother's jeans with visible effort. She has to leave the top button undone. "You see? Perfect fit!"

"You think you should have everything you want."

Valentina flops next to Marcela on the couch and scrunches uncomfortably close, her breath hot on Marcela's neck. "And you are *one cool cucumber,*" she whispers in unsteady English. "*One smooth operator.*"

Marcela almost laughs, but Valentina pokes her arm and hisses. "I deserve these jeans because I lived with our mother for the entire fourteen years I've been alive. I had to identify her dead body. What have you had to do?"

She has had to move back and forth between this world and her own, that's what. She is the one their mother left behind in Boston. But Marcela doesn't say this, because no, she did not have to identify their mother's body, crushed by metal from her car and from the rock of a washed-out road. Marcela can't imagine what that was like and is afraid to ask. Valentina turns on the television and begins to flip through the channels mindlessly.

From the kitchen, Marcela can hear their grandmother's knife—chopping potatoes for ajiaco. Marcela says, "The earrings you're wearing—I'd like them back."

Valentina brushes her long, dark hair away from her ear, revealing a turquoise teardrop earring, something Marcela's father bought on a business trip in Arizona. "I thought they looked prettier on me."

"And my iPod?"

"Haven't seen it."

Their grandmother appears next to the television, straight and silent, her eyes red from days of crying. "Enough," she says. She holds her hand out, and Valentina passes her a box of tissues. "You're at university, Marcela. Be the adult." She looks at Valentina. "Valen, darling. Listen to me. Marcela is your only sister, and she's leaving soon. She doesn't realize it now, but she loves you, even though you steal from her, you nasty little thief."

When Abuela is back in the kitchen, Valentina hunches her

shoulders in imitation. "Be the adult," she whispers, then rolls her eyes at Marcela. Suddenly, Marcela smiles, unable to help herself, and Valentina smiles too. Her hair spills over her shoulders, and she looks beautiful, like their mother in old pictures.

Marcela is on the verge of making a conciliatory remark when Valentina whispers in her ear: "I wish you were leaving sooner."

Marcela is relieved when her sister has to go to work, because this is her chance to go through Valentina's drawers, reclaim her iPod from between crisp school blouses, and take the jeans, which she hides under her mattress. She is not convinced that Valentina won't look for the jeans there, but it's the best place she can think of.

Later, because she has to get out of the cramped apartment, Marcela walks around the boutiques and stalls of the pedestrianized Zona Rosa, wondering what her life would be like if her mother had not returned to Colombia to care for Marcela's ailing grandfather. The trip was meant to be temporary, but she had fallen in love with Valentina's father. Marcela has always wondered why her mother didn't send for her. She could have spent summers with her father and Stephanie instead, they would be in less control of her life, she would feel more at home here in Bogotá, her Spanish would be better. But probably she and Valentina would still hate each other. Abuela is right about a lot of things, but not about her feelings for Valentina; Valentina is impossible to love.

Marcela stops at a stall selling leather goods; the impetus to buy a Christmas gift for her father is automatic, even though no one would expect her to return from her mother's funeral with souvenirs. She sees a belt that would not offend her father's ordinary tastes: plain and black.

Though her hair is almost blonde and the man who makes the belts calls her a gringa, he gives her a good deal because, he says, she speaks okay Spanish. Paying, she spots a small painting of the Virgin Mary next to the box where the vendor keeps his money. Marcela has never been much interested in Catholicism, but she has been surrounded by rosaries this week; at the funeral she stared at the baroque altar, the marble columns, the crying virgin—so that she would not have to look at the weeping men and women around her. Relatives she hardly knows.

This Virgin's face is pretty and wise; she looks calmly into the face of the sleeping infant in her arms. Abuela would like this painting. Poor Abuela, bereft of her daughter, burdened by her squabbling grandchildren, this cold and unfamiliar American girl.

"How much for Mary?" she asks.

The man looks at her, unsmiling. "She's not for sale," he says. "And she's not Mary, but Our Lady of Guazá."

"Who?"

"Patron Saint of Miners. My brother works in the salt mine in Zipaquirá. You can find her there, in the cathedral made from the old salt mine."

By the time Marcela returns home it is almost dinner time, and Valentina is still at her father's downtown electrical appliance store. Abuela shakes her head. "Works too hard when she should be doing her homework," she says. "Every weekend. Organizes all his books! The worst thing is his new girlfriend is a child practically herself."

In the bedroom she shares with Valentina, Marcela lies on her springy mattress and thinks she can feel the shape of the jeans pressed beneath her. She doesn't actually remember seeing her mother wear them; that had been a lie. But she would like to have such memories: what her mother wore for special occasions, what she liked to eat when she lived in the U.S.

Marcela once asked her mother what she had seen in Valentina's father. This was long after he'd left her for someone else—and she said he had reminded her what it felt like to be at home. And then she turned away, back to whatever she'd been doing—drying a dish or folding a dress—and Marcela felt she'd been reprimanded, but she wasn't sure what for.

What would she do if she had more time here? Rent a car and see the country? Visit relatives in Bucaramanga? Through her college, she could arrange to study at a university for a semester; her comparative literature professor suggested this when he heard her mother lived in Bogotá. But Marcela realizes that she, like Valentina, wishes she were leaving sooner.

Her grandmother startles Marcela out of her thoughts by sitting on the bed. "What are your plans for tomorrow?" she asks.

Marcela has no plans. But looking at Abuela's grief-stricken face, this feels like a self-indulgent thing to say. Maybe Abuela wants to spend time together before her departure. "I thought I would visit the Salt Cathedral. Would you like to go?"

"Valentina does not work tomorrow. Take her with you."

"Valentina won't want to come."

"No, but she'll go and be glad. Who knows when you will return. Or if?"

Marcela shakes her head. But she's not actually sure she wants to come back here, ever. Her parents' custody agreement means nothing now, and she's an adult anyway; Abuela said so herself. "I will always come to see you," Marcela says.

"And your sister."

"Yes," Marcela says, just as she hears the door to the apartment open and Valentina's unmistakable sigh. "Of course."

She had imagined the church where the funeral was held, but pillared with white salt instead of gold and marble. A sort of whimsical confection. Only upon arriving at the mountain in Zipaquirá does she realize what this sight-seeing really entails: she and Valentina must descend with hundreds of people 600 feet into the earth. It's a disturbingly morbid activity to undertake so soon after her mother's death. But it is also something to do, so she buys their tickets and joins Valentina in the long line near a tall cement cross that marks the entrance to the mountain.

A misty rain begins, Valentina groans, and scores of black umbrellas open in front of and in back of Marcela and Valentina, a trail, like the dark scales of a long serpent twisting its way down the hill, toward the red-tiled roofs of the village.

"We should have gone to the mall," Valentina says.

Inside, they are greeted by the smell of sulfur, by darkness, by pools of water that collect in corners and reflect the lights placed low on the damp cavern walls.

Their guide wears a miner's yellow hard hat, but her face looks scrubbed and rosy, even in the dim cavern lights. She explains the history: decades ago, miners began to carve altars into the caves from which they excavated tons of salt. These men dedicated their prayers to La Virgen del Rosario de Guazá.

As they pass austere chapels, no longer created by the miners but by artists to represent the stations of the cross, Marcela can picture those original worshippers: leaving flowers for La Virgen on damp rock walls, carrying rosaries in their mouths through chambers passable only on hands and bellies.

Glancing at Valentina spoils her satisfyingly somber mood. "You took it again!" She reaches over to yank the earphones out of her sister's ears. "Anyway, you shouldn't listen to music in here."

"Oooo. Will Jesus be angry?" Valentina holds her hands on either side of her mouth in mock horror, then points heavenward and whispers. "Listen to this shit. That would piss me off if I were Jesus."

Marcela strains to hear: "Ave Maria," sung by digitally enhanced monks and accompanied by wind noise. More haunted house than church, as though they are about to be grabbed by a disembodied hand. She has to admit, it's awful.

They're standing with their group at a balcony carved straight from the mountain. The cavern extends below and in front of them, a mineshaft lit by blue lights planted in the ground and in the walls, shrinking at the far end to a dark point—a hole that leads deeper, connecting, Marcela imagines, to the part of the mountain that still functions as a mine. If she listened carefully, beneath "Ave Maria," she might even hear the clink of hammers, the cracking of the earth.

Some people are tossing coins into the dark.

Valentina waves her arm over the drop. "Do you have any?"

Marcela digs in her pocket and hands a few coins to Valentina, who returns one to Marcela's palm. "Make a wish," she says. She closes her eyes and throws her coin. "Your turn."

But Marcela has never been able to think of the thing she wants when it's time to wish for it, so before she formulates a thought, an expression of all that she desires in that moment, she has tossed the coin into the mineshaft, wishing for nothing but her mother's stupid jeans, which she already has.

She loses her group, she loses Valentina. After wandering, she finally finds her sister sitting on a kneeling stone in a stark, empty chapel. Slicing through the gloom, white light emanates from a towering cross, carved so deeply into the rock that it makes its own tall and narrow cavern. The look on Valentina's face is familiar: bored, angry, calculating.

The sound of heavy boots on stone and rustling paper makes Marcela turn: A flame-haired woman squinting at a pamphlet, fumbling with her glasses. A man stands close to the entrance. In American-accented English, the woman says, "Well, Raymond, this one's supposed to be when they took away His clothes." She looks at Marcela. "You have the right idea, dear, sitting there, contemplating His awesomeness."

This woman is irritating, and Valentina probably connects Marcela with her, an American who makes assumptions. In Spanish, her eyes glassy, her voice flat, she says, "God is dead."

Valentina giggles as the pair leaves. "Shit, gringos are stupid," she says. And before Marcela can come to the defense of herself, if not the tourists, Valentina is pointing to the cross, her expression dark again. "Go in there," she demands.

"What? No."

Valentina pushes Marcela toward the hollowed-out rock and salt that forms the cross. Marcela feels off balance, ready to fall, but then her back touches the wall, and she is engulfed in brightness from the lights planted in the base and sides of the cross. Beyond this brightness, Valentina is a vague and menacing shadow.

"Close your eyes, *cool cucumber*. Relax."

"For a younger sister, you are very bossy."

"Imagine you're in the wall. You are part of the mountain."

"This is weird."

Suddenly, Valentina squeezes next to Marcela, turning Marcela until they face each other, each of their backs pressed now against the sides of the cross. Without warning, Valentina wraps her arms around Marcela's waist, and though Marcela tries peeling them off, Valentina's grip is firm.

"My eyes are closed," Valentina says. "Are yours?"

They aren't but Marcela says, "Yes."

"Imagine, Marcela, we are in a coffin." She crushes her face against Marcela's arm. "What if we were buried alive?" She mumbles into Marcela's sweater. "Like all the miners who have died in the mountain?"

Valentina must be pulling her leg. But when she lifts her head, Marcela sees tears in her sister's eyes.

A memory returns: sharing a bed with her sister—summer evenings when Valentina's father slept over and Abuela stayed in Valentina's bed. Huddled together in the dark room, Valentina's small body curled under Marcela's arm, Marcela sometimes covered her sister's ears to drown out the moaning that came through the wall. Sometimes she woke in the middle of the night to Valentina's hand wrapped tightly around her fingers.

Marcela is finally able to disentangle herself just as a guide leads a group into the chapel.

A woman steps toward them. "You want me to take your picture?"

Valentina gives Marcela a quick shove forward.

"No, no," Marcela says, stepping out of the hollowed wall. As she blinks, adjusting back to darkness, Valentina has slipped past her and back into the main tunnel.

The crowd carries Marcela forward. She passes beneath a domed ceiling, lit by blue lights. Strange planetarium. Instead of stars and clouds, there are the swirling patterns in the rock, veins of salt.

At the bottom of a hand-carved staircase, Marcela stands at a balcony, gazing into the main nave of the church. Below is the tallest cross in the world, 145 feet high, lit from the inside. She feels suddenly cold, realizing for the first time that her jeans are still wet from the rain. Around her, people are praying and taking pictures, kissing each other and looking at their cell phones. She tries to conjure the awe one should feel in a place of worship, but she finds this place so strange—smelly like eggs; sad, but trying hard to be grand and meaningful. Disneyland for grownup Catholics.

At the front of the gallery, she feels Valentina's chin digging into her shoulder. "I'll tell you what I used to wish for when I was a kid," she says. "I wanted your father to be my father."

"What for?" Valentina would hate living with her father and Stephanie! Valentina thinks American parties are like boring meetings? Well, growing up with her father and Stephanie has been like one, never-ending meeting about her grades and life goals.

"I wanted to live in the United States. You always had such nice things."

"You had our mother."

They look at one another for a long time, and to Marcela it seems that perhaps she has said something wrong and offensive because Valentina's gaze turns stormy.

"As soon as you would go back to your father, she would do nothing but watch television all day for weeks." Her long hair shields her face. "I miss her," Valentina says. "Now I'm an orphan."

"That's ridiculous. Your father is still alive."

"He's too busy paying attention to his new girlfriend. Who, by the way, is the same age as you."

Nineteen—their mother's age when she met Marcela's father on a beach in Cartagena. Too young to marry a gringo and move to cold Boston, where she knew no one.

Clutching at the damp, salty wall for support, Marcela follows Valentina down the unlit staircase that leads to the nave. They end up at three narrow doorways.

Valentina scowls. "You know what his girlfriend wanted for her birthday?"

Marcela shakes her head.

"Boobs. My father bought this chick bigger boobs." Valentina shakes her head. "He hates hospitals, so I had to meet her after the surgery to take her home. Can you picture her? My height with dyed-blonde hair? I had to hold her up as we walked to the taxi. Her new chest put her off-balance. One time I let her go, just so I could see her wobble."

Valentina laughs, but Marcela has never seen her sister look more furious. Even when they were fighting about their mother's jeans, Valentina's mouth did not get all tight like this, as if she were about to bite.

A guide is explaining how to choose the right door: the first is for hardened sinners, the second for the average person trying to lead a decent life, and the third for the person with a perfectly clear conscience. Marcela backs up toward the opposite wall as the crowd around her swarms toward the first door. "We're all sinners!" a voice cries, and they're like a conga line passing through.

Valentina waves at Marcela to follow her through the third door. "We're good people, right?" she says. A little of her mischievous twinkle has returned.

Marcela hesitates. Her last time in Bogotá, she and her mother walked the cobblestone streets of the Candelaria, climbed to the top of Monserrate, the lush, green mountain overlooking a city built mostly of red brick. They barely spoke; Marcela did not know what to say to this woman who was more like a distant relative than her mother. So, looking at the incline they had ascended, and at the ski lift shuttling the lazy or tired to the top, she talked about how her father and Stephanie had encouraged her to learn to ski that winter. She had given in reluctantly—how reluctant she was about many things!—and then sprained her ankle and decided that kind of speed was not for her. Listening, her mother seemed flushed with nostalgia for New England, and she talked about skiing with Marcela's father, how clumsy she felt compared with him, and then she laughed about the first time she drove in the snow, her car skidding and crunching over dirty bits of slush and ice. Without warning, she had pulled Marcela close and begun to weep.

"Are you crying?" Valentina puts her hand on Marcela's damp cheek.

She takes Marcela's hand, and Marcela allows herself to be led through the central nave with its milling tourists. A guide chides those who sit, exhausted, in the pews. "Only the wicked need rest!" she says, laughing.

Halfway up the stairs leading up and out of the mountain, Marcela links her arm through her sister's, the way she sees many girls connected on the streets of Bogotá, even here, in the tunnels.

They hold onto each other and the wall and move along with the throng of people ascending with them.

"You can have our mother's jeans, Valen," Marcela says. "I took them from your drawer yesterday while you were at work." Valentina stops moving, her eyes narrowed. "I'm sorry," Marcela whispers. "They would never fit me anyway."

But Valentina breaks into a brilliant smile, their mother's smile. "It's okay!" she says, letting go to dash up the final steps. Once she has reached the exit, daylight flashing behind her, she hooks her fingers through her belt loops and shouts down the stairwell, "I'm already wearing them!"

How did Marcela not notice before? Because they fit Valentina perfectly, better than yesterday when she had to leave the top button undone. And her jacket covered the pockets. They have looked like ordinary jeans all morning.

Marcela trudges up the remaining stairs to a transformed day—sunny and hot. Valentina greets her sister by spinning slowly, removing her jacket, and wagging her hips to show off the swirls of blue and silver glitter, which sparkle now in the light.

My Husband's Second Wife

A new joyful feeling came over him. . . . it was as if a host of vague but important thoughts burst from some locked-up place and, all rushing towards the same goal, whirled through his head, blinding him with their light.
—Leo Tolstoy, *Anna Karenina*

Delia looked the same. Her gray-black hair was piled attractively on her head, in the style she had favored before marrying my husband. At first she didn't see me as she scooped organic walnuts into a paper bag. She wore a signature dress: long, almost transparent. As she leaned toward the bulk bins, the fabric grazed the floor. I considered the best way to escape unnoticed, but then she turned and caught me in the blaze of her smile.

Delia always had a great smile: shimmering, inclusive. Years ago, before I was married, she was just my neighbor. But even though we were older now (some might say actually old) and our children were graduating from college and having their own kids, even though the man who had been our husband was now married to someone else and living in Texas, I still felt awkward to face her like this: my cart filled with nothing but ice cream, potato chips, and cheap rosé.

"You changed your hair!" she said, alarmed.

I had to think about that. My hair was short, but it had been for a long time. "Two years ago, I think?"

"Well." She appeared to reconsider. "It suits you."

Then she asked about my daughter, my son, the grandchild who was now three.

For my part, I asked dutifully after the twins, who for one long summer had lived with my daughter, their much older sister, because Delia and my husband didn't know what else to do with them. ("Mom, they're so spoiled," my daughter had complained, and I smugly refrained from telling her this pleased me.)

"Oh, same." Delia sighed. "Kitty's living with a terrible boyfriend she'll probably marry. Peter's backpacking in Eastern Europe. Claims he's staying in hostels, but the credit card bills!" She rolled her eyes, glanced appraisingly at my cart.

Though she was probably judging me, I was suddenly filled with goodwill. "You should come to our book club. We're reading all the big Russians." This had been Cynthia Schueren's idea—a year of Dostoyevsky, Chekhov, and Tolstoy—but in front of Delia I claimed our goal proudly, as if it were mine.

That smile again, this time a little apology. Of course she wouldn't come. "I've gone a bit lowbrow," she said. "Only murder mysteries and cookbooks these days."

I hid my disappointment behind a conspiratorial little laugh.

We lived in a college town, full of old hippies. It took a lot of effort not to run into each other. When she and my husband first married, I saw her everywhere, and she was wise enough not to try to make conversation. But our mutual friends were always telling me they thought she was pregnant because of either how she looked (fat or glowing) or what she was eating (everything or only carrots with mustard). They saw such claims as therapeutic gossip, but I felt them as little knives stabbing my throat.

In the store, without this husband-sized wedge between us, Delia and I parted amiably, almost tenderly. She reached for my hand, squeezed it, and I saw that she was still wearing her engagement ring. A ring I once coveted, it had belonged to my mother-in-law, who had said gazing at jewelry filled her with the kind of pleasure no man could ever provide.

Over dinner, I told Hugh about running into Delia.

"I thought she and Sam moved to Texas?"

"That's the new wife," I said, "the one who sells insurance."

I didn't know much about her except that she was a former competitive tennis player and, according to my son, "older than you'd expect for a third wife."

"Delia was the voracious reader?"

Frankly, it surprised me that Hugh remembered that much. "Apparently she isn't anymore," I informed him.

Hugh did not pick up on my tone of surprise. So we moved on to other topics: the group of senior citizens—"Our near future," Hugh said—to whom he was teaching computer literacy at the community center. Also a couple of my patients whose troubles I wasn't supposed to talk about, so I made sure not to use their names. Hugh and I had been together for seventeen years and had never married.

In the evening, we undressed each other slowly. Hugh always smiles when I kiss his eyelids, the inside of his wrists. Our hunger is familiar and easily satisfied. After, we read together in bed.

In a week, my book group was meeting to talk about *Anna Karenina*. What I had failed to mention to Delia was how slow the reading was for me. I couldn't keep all the Russian names straight, and this alone felt like a personal failing. Mostly, I didn't want to admit that I kind of hated the book she had tried to get me to read for years. I wanted to hold up my reading as a kind of triumph. But of what? If Delia no longer read and loved the big Russians writers, what kind of triumph would it be to finish *Anna Karenina*, and then tell her about it?

In bed, the pages inches from my face, the words just swam together, and in front of me I could only see Delia.

Once upon a time, Delia adored Tolstoy. She tried to push *Anna Karenina* on me the way my evangelical neighbor had tried to push Jesus on my daughter when she was young. (Though we're Jewish, the neighbor assured my daughter she still had time to accept Christ into her heart.)

The first time Delia encouraged me to read it, I laughed. "I'm not sure I identify with a woman throwing herself in front of a train."

"Tolstoy's genius is that you *will* identify with her—and all the other characters too." She had smiled, but I felt like she was chastising me, and for this reason alone I had stayed away from the book with the stubbornness of a teenager.

"And really," Delia had continued, "That's a small part of the story. It's a shame that's all anyone knows about it."

Delia used to say she was drawn to what she called the *purple density* of Russian prose. "Russian writers make you appreciate the complexities of people, the sorrow and magic of being a dull little human on planet earth."

To be clear, it wasn't just the Russians Delia loved. She read everything from Murdoch to Murakami and remembered every character, every storyline. She could describe the atmosphere of a book on a molecular level, as if she'd experienced it. As if she'd created it herself.

I still remember my husband talking about that quality with deep affection. He was plucking the white hairs out of his beard, after one of Delia's parties, and I had to pause as I unhooked my bra. It was my first inkling of a defection.

Delia taught high school English, and every wall of her house was covered with novels. Inside each book the margins were filled with copious notes in Delia's tiny, perfect penmanship. As for the physical differences, I was on the short side and once very thin. Delia was tall, queenly, and generously padded.

I understood that my husband was in love with her at a New Year's party she hosted at her rambling farmhouse in the mid '80s. As we all hugged goodbye at her door, I observed how he held on to her, I could see in his fingertips how he wanted to cling to her flesh.

And I didn't blame him exactly. When he finally confessed his feelings to me, my first reaction was of regret—that I wouldn't be on the receiving end of Delia's embrace anymore, or of her genuine, glittery smile.

Only later did I feel rage. But I expressed my anger quietly, in the dark of our bedroom, so that the children wouldn't hear fighting in their dreams.

"If you love her more than me," I hissed, "then go." It sounded like something I'd heard in a movie once, and I immediately regretted saying it.

Yet it did have some effect, because he embraced me then, weeping into my breasts, which he kissed and admired, working himself up as if to thank me for my understanding. I could feel that the tension had gone out of him, that he wept only out of relief, that he caressed me as if in a distant memory of me and my body.

Afterwards he dressed quickly, and then he went. Willingly, eagerly, straight to Delia's bed.

Delia never gave our husband a clichéd ultimatum. According to friends, when he told her about the woman in Texas, whom he had met in an airport security line, Delia merely remarked how much she would miss his hair. (He had all of it, and it gave him an appealing illusion of youth and vigor.) Then while he was at work, she piled his things neatly in boxes, including any book he had ever given her, and left them outside in the rain. She changed the locks on the house, which was still her house anyway. They'd never put his name on the deed.

When he knocked on the door, she laughed at him from the window of her study.

He pleaded: "I love you, I love you, forgive me."

I think he might have stayed. He had never thrived in hot weather. But at that moment I believe Delia saw in him both the man she and I had loved at the same time and the man who would one day merely be the father of her difficult adult children. She closed the window.

When my mother-in-law was feeling blue, she liked to spread out her rings and necklaces on the dining room table. On a chilly evening, weeks before I married her son, she was in one of these moods, and she poured cocktails for each of us, which we drank while she told me the story behind each ring, each necklace, every antique brooch and hat pin. They were family jewels, and the ring that would one day be Delia's stood out from the rest: a delicate platinum setting with indigo sapphires on either side of a large, sparkling diamond.

The ring had traveled all the way from Belarus a century earlier, sewn into a young bride's petticoat. My mother-in-law's own mother had worn it casually, while doing the dishes.

As soon as I saw it, I understood what my mother-in-law meant about the pleasure of exquisite possessions. Everything else in the room faded, and I felt a warm, new space open up in my chest.

My mother-in-law suggested I try it on. My fingers were too small, and the ring slid around. She smiled kindly. On her left hand, her ring and pinky fingers were little nubs, down to the knuckles, a birth defect she never hid. Instead, she had adorned that hand with beloved rings, ever since my husband was a child and easily embarrassed.

"Let's find something more fitting for you," she said. She tugged the ring off my hand easily and dug out from a silk bag a smaller one: a slim gold band, with a tiny, dusky stone at the center. It fit perfectly, and I accepted it reluctantly.

In the middle of the night, Hugh snoring peacefully beside me, I woke up thinking about the ring—not my old one, but Delia's.

Why did Delia still wear it? Perhaps because she still loved my husband a little, as I had for a while after he left.

Knowing Delia, I think she just realized what the ring was worth.

The weekend stretched out pleasantly for me and Hugh. We began Saturday morning with what my daughter calls our "bougey-white-couple-ritual": walk to our favorite coffee shop, meander the farmers market to buy cheese and flowers, end up at home with the newspaper on our laps for the entire afternoon. I let my daughter tease us because she's right. I have the life I want, and I have no illusions; I'm very lucky to be a dull little human on this sorrowful, magical planet.

At home, I made another pot of coffee while Hugh arranged the gladiolusesas in a vase he'd brought into our home from his previous marriage. It's made of a humble-blue clay, and any flowers that sit in it seem to explode with the vividness of triumphant fireworks. Watching him cut the stems of the flowers, I felt warm and happy.

But underneath this pleasant feeling was an anxiety I was not quite used to anymore. I'd practically held my breath during our morning walk through the market, suspecting we'd run into Delia, now that I'd seen her again after so long. We didn't see her, but now, from there on the dining room table, *Anna Karenina* loomed up at me, a thick brick of accusation.

In addition to being a fan of expensive jewelry, my mother-in-law loved a good gut feeling. She claimed she'd known JFK was not long for this world the day of his inauguration. ("It was the way he looked at Jackie," she said, "as if from very far away.") Regarding the caterer I wanted to choose for the wedding because of an article in the local paper, my mother-in-law suggested her cake would be beautiful but disappointing. ("That woman does not look as if she has ever enjoyed eating.") Two days before my wedding day, she stopped by my apartment without calling ahead, something she only did when she had something important to tell me—or warn me about.

As it happened, I had company. A college friend who'd been invited to the wedding. He'd driven back to town early to suggest I might be making a terrible mistake by getting married to a man we both knew as predictable and stubborn.

This friend was handsome in a boyish way I'd always over-looked but suddenly found appealing. As I described the quietness of my current life, I felt a new recognition set in: that I'd been going through the motions with my soon-to-be-husband, not fully living in my body. My friend gazed at my lips while I talked. When he touched my hand as I poured his third glass of wine, pleasant chills shot through my limbs. Then he declared his love for me over my famous lasagna. He said he'd always loved me, in fact.

Nothing this dramatic had ever happened to me. I was swept right off my lukewarm feet and out of my clothes. It didn't occur to me until later that I was trying on a more glittery role just to see how it suited me.

My old friend and I were finished and staring awkwardly into each other's eyes when the doorbell rang and my mother-in-law called my name from the hall. Her voice became more urgent, and it filled me with dread. I didn't answer.

The passion that had so recently consumed me drained quickly from my body, leaving room for guilt. As well as a surging repulsion for the man lying smugly in my bed.

Even though I now knew with every part of me that it was a terrible idea, I informed him I would be getting married as planned, and he didn't try to argue.

At my reception, after the delicious cake had been obliterated and the dance floor had been waltzed upon, as I thought blearily about the man I had considered running off with two days before and who was now dancing languidly with my cousin Jenny, my mother-in-law plunked herself down in the seat next to me and proceeded to tell me why she'd stopped by my apartment:

She had decided I should have the ring I'd loved after all. And that she would have it re-sized for my finger.

"It came to me in a dream," she said, "that you deserve it more than anyone." Her voice was urgent, but her smile was tense with worry. "In the dream you were alone on one of those horrible, tasteless cruise ships. You were crying on the deck, and I was calling to you from shore."

Again I was consumed with guilt.

"I think you should hold on to the ring a bit longer," I said, patting her own ring-bound fingers. I imagined I would earn it back, with my faithfulness to her son. She would sense when the time had come.

Her face relaxed.

"You know the funniest thing happened after I knocked on your door," she said.

"Oh?" My heart thudded, but it wasn't what I expected.

"Your neighbor came out to see what the fuss was about. What a stunning woman! I told her I was certain I'd met her before, but now I think that's because she reminds me of Greta Garbo. I liked her very much. I think you and Sam will too."

The stunning neighbor was Delia. Until my mother-in-law pointed her out, I'd barely noticed her—she was the kind of woman who blended in until she didn't blend at all.

After college, my daughter lived for a year in France, working as a nanny. She returned home with a view of Americans that has stuck around family conversation: we're particularly selfish, self-absorbed, and narrow-minded. I do not disagree. What I tell my daughter, when we talk about these things, is that we're also very good at punishing ourselves; I don't mean our criminal justice system—*that* is a national embarrassment and tragedy—I mean we create arbitrary, individual standards and hate ourselves when we can't live up to them.

Hugh was already deep into the arts section, and I had the crossword in front of me. But I sighed and hefted my assigned reading from the table into my lap.

Hugh chuckled.

"Something funny?" I said.

He shook his head, his brown eyes soft and understanding. "Just admiring your struggle."

Without comment, I lugged *Anna Karenina* up to my face. We were in the countryside. Levin was mowing his field and enjoying it. Immediately began this little internal back-and-forth: It's an important book, and I should know about it. Also: I am a grown woman, and life is short; I should be able to read whatever the hell I want.

I put the book back down, reached for my phone, and Googled Tolstoy. (Americans are also very good at distracting themselves.)

For minutes or hours, I disappeared into a Tolstoy-internet rabbit hole and resurfaced, feeling indignant.

"Hugh, did you know Tolstoy could not have written his books without his wife, who not only raised their children pretty much single-handedly, she stayed up late at night—while he slept—to transcribe his practically illegible scribbles?"

"Hmmm," Hugh mumbled.

Clearly, that line of thinking wasn't going anywhere on a beautiful Saturday morning, reserved for the joys of leisure. Hugh is endlessly patient and kind, and often very funny. But our talk tends to maintain a steady level, while in my conversations with women there's always a satisfying energy thrumming below the surface, one that pushes us toward each other, diminishing any separation between us.

I couldn't stop myself from wondering if Delia might find the story of Tolstoy's burdened wife more interesting.

Delia raised Peter and Kitty pretty much on her own, even while she was married to my husband. A real estate agent when he and I were married, he was expanding into larger-scale acquisitions—not just single-family homes but land for development—by the time he left me. And he had begun to have a lot of out-of-state business meetings. Of course, Delia couldn't have thought she was snagging a doting family man, at least not if she'd been paying attention all those years she was hanging around our apartment.

After we got married and my husband moved into my small rental, we started inviting Delia over for dinner. She brought her vitality with her, as well as her library, which she loved to lend out to friends so we could talk about "beautiful ideas, not just the weather." My husband loved these get-togethers, where he drank and joked, and made a general impression of charming brilliance while I served the underrated hors d'oeuvres and wiped up wine and coffee spills from our one good rug.

When I became pregnant, Delia was always around. She took enormous interest in my nutrition and regularly brought over "treats" that were packed with the kind of grains she believed our oldest ancestors relied on to maintain good health in harsh climates. I did not buy into dietary ideology, but I'd eat the cookies or nut bars in front of her because, in her presence, they actually took on a superior flavor. Once she was gone, I might as well have been eating cardboard.

It wasn't just the taste of food that Delia altered. She carried a pleasant glow with her into any room, casting aside shadows both real and metaphorical. When my daughter was a newborn and I was a sleep-deprived wraith of my former self, my husband was always working.

He had struggled for years to get his name on For Sale signs across the county, and now that he was a father, he said it was more important than ever to get his "brand imprinted on the landscape." Which meant that he was often gone on weekends and evenings, leaving me with our tiny child and what someone would now probably diagnose as postpartum depression. At least, I reasoned, his business seemed to be picking up, finally.

During this time, Delia dropped by once or twice a week to sit with me and provide adult conversation. She'd rock my baby to sleep so I could take a shower or walk outside alone. She sang lullabies in a soothing tone I never achieved myself, and I'm fairly certain my daughter's perfect pitch is all thanks to Delia, not to me or my husband.

One thing I never told Delia: as much as I loved her company, I was aware of holding something back. Not reading the books she suggested. Throwing away her carob brownies after she'd gone home. I never told her how I cried sometimes when I was alone, or about the lapse before my wedding—though I often thought of my fling while in her company and had a feeling she'd understand.

Delia held back too. Of course she did. She kept perhaps the biggest secret she could have from me. For years I felt sad about what we didn't share.

When I described to Cynthia Schueren this sense of loss, our friendship was new, we were still young (well, middle-aged), and she looked at me steadily. "You shared a husband. Without your permission."

"When you put it that way—"

"When you put it any way, you don't owe Delia sympathy. She's not your client." Cynthia is a lawyer, and right about everything. Still, I thought forgiveness was the best path forward.

"I understand why my husband loved her."

"See, you don't need to do that. You don't always have to be understanding."

I was about to go back into *Anna*, when a text came through from Cynthia:

"I'm in love."

Cynthia is a compassionate woman, infinitely loyal to her wife. But she always has a crush on someone: the handsome butcher who gives her secret discounts, the young woman at the bookstore who always puts the perfect novel in her hands. I waited for her to explain this newest enchantment.

"It's Levin," she wrote. "Levin is my ideal husband."

"I'll take your word for it."

"Take Tolstoy's!" she wrote.

I grimaced at my phone.

I like the women in my book group, but I was initially resistant to the whole idea of it. When Cynthia first invited me, I immediately declined. To me, a book club meant only one thing: a bunch of gossipy old women getting sloshed on wine.

Cynthia had laughed. "You love wine and gossip." She has a mischievous smile. "And you're not getting any younger."

I felt caught out. "Okay," I told her.

I was pleasantly surprised by everyone's commitment to literature. To be sure, there is a lot of drinking and gossiping too, but against a backdrop of intellectual warmth and vigor. We devoted our first year of reading to Edith Wharton, who became *my* literary crush, the second year to bestselling literary fiction. I did not argue with Cynthia when she proposed a year of Russian literature, but I did confess to her, alone, that Delia had been a devotee, and I still had issues when it came to Tolstoy.

Cynthia tried to be kind. She squeezed my hand. "Now, I don't know a lot about Tolstoy, but as far as I understand he didn't write *Anna Fucking Karenina* for Delia, did he?"

I laughed. I shook my head. Oh, how I adored Cynthia for saying that.

But there was still a serious voice, located in the part of my body that held on tightly to stuff it shouldn't, and while I laughed the voice whispered, *Yes*.

When our son was born, my husband wanted to move to a bigger house.

Ultimately though, it was Delia who moved first, to the farm-house she still occupies, and that my husband sold to her. He initially wanted it for us, but I rejected the idea of country living. I suppose they fell in love with each other when he was walking her through its empty rooms, singing its praises. Perhaps she loved him because he loved the house, and perhaps he loved the idea of her living in the place he'd already imagined owning. Of course I didn't piece this together until later, and I'm not even sure I have it absolutely right. I never saw my husband on a tour, but I knew him enough to understand he was at his best when he knew he had a sure thing.

The house is on a lovely, windy hill, looking out over dairy farms and evergreen forests. Since we had just one car in the early days of our marriage, I did not often get out to see Delia with my children.

We bought a house right downtown. I could push the stroller to storytime at the library, and pick up groceries at the co-op, where I would sometimes run into Delia. Running into Delia—before the divorce—was always something the children looked forward to because she kept small gifts for kids in her purse: foreign coins and Mexican Worry Dolls and barrettes she'd made by braiding colorful ribbons. Usually we'd stop for a while to talk over coffee or tea. Leaving her, I'd inevitably feel better than I had before.

Eventually, the children began school. I finished my Master's degree and converted an addition at the back of our house to an office for my private practice. We purchased another car, but I rarely used it, accustomed as I had become to getting around on foot and by bike. Delia began to throw big parties once or twice a year, and I always brought the artichoke dip that she never touched. I had a feeling it annoyed her, my insistence on bringing dairy into her home, and I would be lying if I didn't admit I had derived a small amount of pleasure from her disdain, though at the time I couldn't have actually told you why.

My mother-in-law never again referred to the ring she'd wanted to re-size for me, and I didn't bring it up because I didn't know how. Instead, during those years, and for a while after my husband left, I wore the ring she'd given me. And whenever I looked at it, I thought about beautiful things.

Hugh and I finished the crossword together, and he went outside to his gardening. In the late afternoon, he drove to his daughter's house to spend the evening babysitting his grandchildren, and I relaxed into the luxurious silence of our house.

I held the book in my lap for a full minute before opening it again.

Levin in his fields, Levin in his thoughts. I could still feel myself making an effort to read the words, to follow along with his progress. So many words, when I would think fewer words would do. I couldn't read them without imagining them in Delia's head, I couldn't read them without seeing the images they created as if they'd been created for her. Outside, the clouds rolled in, and I turned on the lamp beside me.

I don't remember when I fell asleep, only waking up to Hugh kissing my forehead and removing the book very gently from my hands.

Days passed. I'd read a page or two a night, and that was it. Each day I woke up with a sense of moral and personal failure.

The morning of our book club meeting, however, I woke up with a raging headache. I cancelled my appointments for the day.

Hugh said, "Do you think it has to do with *Anna Karenina*?"

"Of course it does." The words came out sharp, but truthfully I felt pleased that he was interested in my psychology. "I am quite aware of the power I'm giving to this classic work of literature."

"Too much power," Hugh said, kindly.

"Cynthia would agree."

But after taking a codeine, I sank into bed with my eye mask on with this thought: isn't art meant to be this powerful? Isn't art, when it moves us, one of the few true talismans humans have?

When I woke again, it was almost eleven, Hugh was gone, and so was my headache.

It felt silly at first, but I held a little prayer in my head, the kind of thing I don't really believe but still maybe kind of believe: a counter-curse or opening-of-my-heart mantra. I thought of Delia's sparkling ring. I thought of lighting incense and laughed at myself. As I said, we live in a town of old hippies.

And then I began to read.

In the silence of my house, in the comfort of my bed, Levin's movements and desires took shape. All the words on the page began to come together, very slowly, and then to feel necessary. After a while I forgot I was reading them. I simply disappeared as Levin disappeared into his labor.

By the time Hugh came home, I was late for my book club. There were texts from Cynthia on my phone. It didn't matter. I was still in bed, still reading, sweaty from the humid air and the effort the book was exerting on me. I wasn't finished, but I was, at last, sunk into the world Tolstoy had created.

When I emerged from that world, what a joy to find it now belonged to me. I savored each step while I walked to Cynthia's house, knowing I'd be too late for the discussion but still in time for the wine and gossip. *Anna Karenina* was mine, Tolstoy too. Delia belonged to her cookbooks, her murder mysteries, to my fractured memories—not to me. I allowed myself a good, satisfying minute of deep resentment. The idea that Delia and I had shared anything significant was a pretty and convenient illusion. And I'd used it to keep myself from hating her.

When I ran into her at the grocery store I longed to be able to tell her that—finally—I loved what she'd once loved.

Now that I finally loved it, now that it was mine, I didn't want to tell her at all.

Claire Tells a Story

I always felt relieved to see Claire because she inevitably had a lot on her mind. Talking with her gave me an opportunity to get out of my own head, which was also full but not of useful things, nothing I wanted to discuss with other people. At 34, Claire was tall and striking, the woman everyone watched at a party. She was born in a sunny state to cardiologists who still paid for her phone plan and promised to help with a mortgage on a house, should she ever settle down. One thing I liked about Claire was that she didn't hide her luck. She could admit she was generally happy, even though her life always seemed like an entertaining mess: a series of girlfriends she wanted to marry until they proposed, a boring temp job to pay the rent while she wrote her danceable breakup songs, and a successful younger brother her parents always compared her to.

Whenever I drove into town—which wasn't often anymore—Claire and I met for coffee or lunch, and she would launch right into the latest dilemma. She was a captivating storyteller, with a gift for narrative structure and the perfect, telling detail. Even though another person might have come across as self-absorbed, Claire always managed to pull me right into her life the way my favorite books had as a child.

The last time we met, she was getting over a three-day visit from her parents. They stayed with her and her girlfriend in their tiny apartment and, in spite of Claire's initial fears, the visit began well, with everyone happy to see each other.

Her parents were physically vigorous and enjoyed the outdoors, so Claire and Elise took them canoeing. The bright day cast a general glow over most of the afternoon, during which they had a picnic on the riverbank, with a view of other boaters passing and waving.

As one particularly enthusiastic kayaker wished them well, Claire's mother remarked how friendly Midwesterners are, in comparison with most Americans. That's when Claire noticed her parents giving each other little eyebrow signals, and she immediately felt annoyed.

Her mother and father had always been snobs about the Midwest. When they visited, they came laden with oranges and ripe cheeses, as if Claire lived in a food desert and not a college town full of hipster organic-farmers. And of course there were her Midwestern girlfriends. Claire knew her parents were afraid she might marry one of them instead of the college boyfriend they had preferred (the tall engineer from Stanford) and never move back west.

But as she watched her mother and father, she noticed how warmly they smiled at Elise. And her opinion shifted again. How could they be upset about Elise—beautiful as a fluffy new sweater and responsible with her money?

Claire's next thought, and this was much worse, was that one of them was terminally ill and afraid to tell her in front of Elise, with whom she'd been living for just two months and could hardly be counted as part of the family.

So Claire made a space the next morning to be with her mother and father, while Elise was teaching a water aerobics class to senior citizens at the YMCA. She made breakfast and a huge pot of dark roast coffee for all of them to drink while they read the *Times*. When they all had their newspapers open in front of them, her chest pulsed with happiness at her life: a small but tidy home, a solid relationship, and a job she didn't like but would leave for in an hour like a grownup. In short, she felt the most together she'd ever been around her parents, and prepared for what was to come, even if it meant moving home to help take care of one of them, should that be what they needed.

But that wasn't it at all. When she asked if they were well, her father grimaced. Never been better, he said, his mouth full of oatmeal.

Her mother said, We're about to invest a lot of money in Patagonia, in fact.

For a minute no one spoke. Claire's parents were as attuned to the power of a good pause as she. Finally, she asked what the hell they were talking about.

It turned out that Claire's brother, the successful attorney, had fallen in love with an Argentinian woman while traveling with friends in South America. The woman owned the Patagonian hostel he'd stayed in. He was moving next month to be with her and help run the place.

And help raise her daughter, Claire's father added.

Yes, Claire's mother said, the woman has a child.

Now Claire felt torn. For years, her brother had told her she was wasting her Ivy League education on odd jobs. Yet now he was the one prepared to give up his practice and become part of the business sector he most abhorred, the hospitality industry. On the one hand, Claire was relieved that her parents were healthy and that it was her brother disappointing them for once. On the other hand, she envied him. She hadn't traveled abroad or used her Spanish in years. She had never loved anyone enough to give up everything to be with them. All she'd given up to move in with Elise was a cat she was allergic to anyway.

To make matters worse, her parents had agreed to pay for a lavish wedding in Argentina, a country they'd never visited, so that the woman's family could attend.

Couldn't they try living together first? Immediately, Claire knew it was the wrong question to ask.

Her parents became quiet, and she felt herself falling under the appraising gaze she was more accustomed to.

What about you, they asked. What do you want for your future?

Oh god, she said. Here goes.

This girlfriend, her father said, seems like a keeper to me.

It's too early to tell, Claire said. I just moved in!

And then they plagued her with a series of familiar questions: didn't she want to have a baby one day? A house with an actual guest room? A job she was proud of instead of one where she sat in front of a computer all day and answered phones for people with more influence than her?

At this point in her story, Claire sighed and set down her cup of coffee. The clink of it brought me back into the life around me: the students' faces turned blue by their laptop screens, the grinding of beans behind the counter. My chair felt too solid, and a draft from the nearby door blew meanly at my ankles. Claire smiled her miraculous smile, roused by inhabiting the voices of her disapproving parents.

Anyway, she said, I've talked the whole time. Same old same old, right? She laughed. What about you?

I wanted her to keep talking. Whenever Claire became aware of me not just as an audience but a person with concerns and hungers, the air between us shifted and left me feeling unbalanced and hollow. But to appease her I provided a brief summary of my life that included fractious faculty meetings and of my sensitive child, burdened with hours of homework at the age of seven.

I skimmed over the impending separation from my husband, my insomnia, and the great surges of emotion that sometimes left me weeping stupidly in my office with the door closed and locked. Not because I didn't want Claire to know, but because it bored me to talk about.

Eventually I turned the conversation back to Claire. Would she bring Elise to her brother's wedding in Argentina?

Claire shook her head. She'd decided to take the opportunity to travel for a few months, be alone, and write new songs inspired by the people and landscape of South America. There's nothing keeping me here, when it comes down to it. She looked around the little café as if were suddenly provincial.

My drive home came as a relief—an hour between the mainland of my old friendship and the island of my home, which, in the ways of islands, left me feeling isolated from former versions of myself. Once upon a time, hadn't those selves wanted the things I currently possessed?

My husband never liked Claire. He found her flakey, and it was true she sometimes canceled plans at the last minute. What we couldn't agree about were Claire's stories, which my husband described as trivial. This slight bothered me as much as if I'd told the stories myself. How could I convey to him the power Claire had, the joy she provided? As I held her in my head, her voice rising and falling in imitation of her parents, her girlfriend, the new sister-in-law she could already imagine befriending, I felt the satisfaction of the child whose bedtime story is not yet complete, who will go on listening to the words until her eyes are closed, until she is asleep and dreaming peacefully.

The All Clear

1

When the tornado sirens started, my husband and I were on our front porch, watching the storm. He'd just strapped towels to our car, to protect it from hail. This was March, and the grass was already green from an abnormally warm winter followed by days of rain. I was eight months pregnant with our first child.

Gently, Wes took my hand. "We should head inside, into the basement."

We'd never heeded the sirens before. The spring storms had always passed us by.

Obviously, circumstances were different. We stayed in the basement that night for three hours. For a while we just stood on tiptoe to look at the world through the small window at the foot of the stairs. Branches blowing up the street. Pieces of paper set loose from the recycling bin. And the sky whirling and shifting: gray to gray-black, edges blurring yellow. What we were waiting for was that eerie green shade, the color of danger.

Eventually, we got tired of looking, but Wes said it wasn't safe yet to go upstairs. The sirens were still sounding regularly enough to remind us.

I felt agitated more than scared. Lately, I constantly worried about time's passing. How I'd never complete what I wanted to before the baby was born. Not that I believed "famous rich painter" was even a thing anymore. But there were still a number of paintings I had ideas for, and yet no energy to complete them. Every night when I got home from work, I collapsed on the couch and napped for an hour until dinner, after which I went to bed for real.

Now here we were in the basement with nothing but boxes filled with castoffs that Wes and I had accumulated over the five years we'd lived in the house.

"We should at least sort through this junk," I suggested in the manner of someone more efficient, and so we started digging through boxes and marveling at our terrible memory for our possessions.

Some things we'd very much wanted to possess, in fact: an espresso maker, a stained-glass lamp, a set of unused dishes someone had given to us on our wedding day. We made a pile of all the things we could sell at a garage sale once the weather improved.

The basement was your average Midwest basement, cold and damp and prone to flooding. All our belongings were on pallets or metal shelves.

On one of those shelves, I found a portfolio bulging with old drawings and sketchbooks, all of them from college, and as I sifted through the stack, Wes looked up from a plastic tub of camping gear. We hadn't gone camping since 1999, when we lived near mountains, not plains. Earthquakes instead of tornadoes.

"Are you sure you want to do that?" he said.

He knew how I got when I looked through old work. Like a sad drunk who sits at the bar until the wee hours of the morning, slumping into her bottomless bourbon. Things I once made always struck me as little, unexplored gems—proof of a former, unrealized talent. I was usually reluctant to say unrealized genius, though this phrase sometimes floated up to the surface, a tempting but inaccurate lure and anchor.

I ignored Wes and continued sifting, continued sinking. A

self-portrait (a decent, melancholy likeness); doodles of unsuspecting café-goers in Rome, where I had studied abroad; an accomplished sketch of my Italian landlord's fat cat, who used to sit on my balcony to sun herself.

Already, I could feel the effects: a hardening in my chest, a gradual separation from my present body as I slipped back into the former hand making these marks, the former eye seeing and responding to that former world. I'd never been somewhere so old, where I was at once entirely trivial and actually alive for the very first time. With senses I had never used so well before to smell, to taste, to see, to touch.

"That's a pretty one."

Wes had come up behind me and was gazing with me at a series of hands drawn in charcoal—open, closed, holding a lit cigarette. "For Noah," it said at the bottom, in my handwriting.

"Old boyfriend?" His voice arrived from very far away. Teasing, kind, wary.

"I think I'd remember that sort of thing."

The words came out a little touchy, but Wes put his arms around me, around my stomach, and that way I began my resurfacing. The baby kicked, and we both felt it. He backed away, returned to the camping gear.

I almost suspected someone else of having made these assured drawings. My Italian roommate, perhaps. She had always been in love with someone. We used to sit for hours in the kitchen of our San Lorenzo apartment, talking about boys and girls we flirted and slept with while we drew each other and drank wine.

But when I turned the page in the sketchbook, a card slipped out, one made of plain old printer paper, the dot matrix kind with the perforated edges. The card was blank on the front, except for an unremarkable heart (drawn in blue ink), and on the inside, this inscription: "Liz, thank you for being an example of ways I wish to be. Love, Noah."

Such a strange little sentence of gratitude. How had he wished to be? In what ways had I been an example? Though proof of me knowing a Noah, and him knowing me, it failed to jog any image of the man, aside from the vague likelihood of a beard.

2

We never lost power. Eventually, the sirens stopped and the wind quieted. We put our flashlights away and went upstairs. It was still light out—lighter, even, than hours before, because the storm had passed and it wasn't even dinnertime.

Wes wanted to check on the car. The infant seat was already in the back, ready for an early arrival. We pushed open the front door and stepped onto the porch. The air was pleasantly cool, the sky radiant. I expected to see rainbows shooting across our lawn. We didn't yet know that several miles up the road, the tornado had touched down, wrenched up a row of wooden houses, scattered them elsewhere.

At first we could see only a mild disarray: bits of trash scattered in the yard, a telephone wire sagging over the street. But in a moment Wes was muttering, running. A large branch from the old black walnut tree had fallen on the hood of the car, crushing the metal and front headlight and sending whispery little cracks across the windshield.

Wes gaped down at the mess, then looked up at me, helplessly. "Well, shit. This is going nowhere pretty fast."

3

Noah's car is a white Saab with a badly dented front fender. On the way to the airport, he holds a cigarette out his open window, even though it's raining.

I'm in danger of missing my plane, but he drives slowly, reluctantly. We've known each other a matter of hours; we met at the last-minute going-away party my roommate held for me. I never learn who invited him. He's older, not a student. A carpenter or contractor. Recently heartbroken. Or anyway: lonely but not desperate. At the party, he admired the sketches I'd hung up on the kitchen walls. Because I felt flattered, and because he seemed to be the only one not drinking, I asked him for a ride.

On the way he tells me he once dreamed of being a sculptor. He says he'll show me his work when I return in ten months. For the first time in years, he says, he has some new ideas. He gives me his address on a receipt he pulls from his wallet.

From my new city I write him a letter; he replies with a card. I draw a picture for him but am reluctant to send it, perhaps because looking at it reminds me of the thrill of being admired.

In Rome, I live under tall ceilings; I am reborn. Speaking Italian. Drinking espresso, painting every afternoon in a perfect, decrepit little studio.

Vivere senza rimpianti is something I become too fond of saying.

Absorbed by the world and happy in its firm-but-fleeting grasp, I give away most of what I make: nudes sketched in my morning classes, the narrow alleys and sloping hills of Travestere, the shifting light on my own hands as they work.

Possibly the drawings and paintings were beautiful, possibly they were amateurish and dull.

Now I wish I had kept them all.

The End of the Workshop

For the first evening of class, The Professor asked his new graduate students to bring in one page of their favorite piece of writing. The students had to prepare a little presentation about why they'd chosen the piece and that particular writer. The Professor had been giving this assignment for over two decades, and he had liked it initially because the students liked it, and because it often informed their discussions for the rest of the semester. But the reason he still liked the assignment was because he no longer listened while the students talked, and the three-hour class passed by without him needing to prepare anything in advance.

Because he did not listen, he had no sense of how hard each of these new students had deliberated over which writer to talk about. They wanted their responses to feel genuine, yet smart. They wanted their admiration to feel real, and to inspire admiration in their classmates and in their professor too.

He was not famous, and yet they still believed he was powerful. He had the largest office of all the faculty, and the nicest classroom, with wood-paneled walls and a large, round wooden desk. All of their other classes were in narrow, fluorescent-lit classrooms, at tables they could barely all fit around.

The students did not yet know that this professor did not care who their favorite writers were, but it would soon become clear.

What these students would also learn, from graduate students who had been in the program longer, was that The Professor had once been almost famous but had been discovered, after his first successful book, to have little actual talent beyond seeing a manuscript through from beginning to end. (A talent they would, themselves, appreciate in a few years.) And so he feared the talent of others.

The talent of his male students, that is. As for the talent in his female students—he did not fear that at all, because he did not see it. He believed that eventually his female students would marry and have children and possibly teach writing in college, maybe even publish a book or two that would sit quietly on the shelf of a used bookstore somewhere in the country, next to other unremarkable novels by women and forgettable men. If he knew one true thing about his female students, it was that they would never be called geniuses.

One of his female students was talking now about the writer she most admired. Outside the tall windows, the sky took on a burning, golden hue. For the first time that evening, The Professor kind of listened. This student was very pretty. Not especially young—thirties, he guessed, but she had the look he liked: pale, full mouth, dark and thoughtful eyes, the kind of face that was approachable, smiled easily, and was therefore also unlikely to tell him to fuck off.

Hearing the name of the writer she admired—a woman, a contemporary of his (English, not American)—he let out a chuckle.

The pretty student stopped talking. "Excuse me?" she said.

She looked confused, poor girl. In his most gallant voice he said, "Please. Continue."

She did. She read the page from one of this writer's novels—not the most famous one, and not one The Professor had read, but one he knew about. The other students seemed to murmur in admiration of the writing. They laughed at the funny bits. He did not laugh, because he did not find the bits funny.

Usually, on a first day of workshop he'd simply watch the pretty students' mouths. He'd allow his eyes to settle on a girl's breasts, then imagine what it would be like to fuck her. Before fucking her, he might first tell her about the many students he'd slept with in his distant past. "Oh! You don't believe me, but I still have their love letters!" he would say, and it was all true. He knew he looked old to them. But once he'd been young and handsome and everyone had said he was going to be the next Great American Novelist.

Normally, he'd allow himself to simply drift away into these pleasant memories, but tonight he felt a new and unexpected irritation behind his eyes. The writer this girl loved—there was no other way of saying it—was famous. Revered even, in some literary circles. And not just as a fiction writer, but as a philosopher. She was a Dame, in fact, and he had once met her at a conference at Harvard. Quite a handsome woman, good figure. But an unattractive haircut, totally unbecoming and boyish. While drinking her glass of bourbon (neat), she had looked past him, through him, and addressed all her remarks to Seamus Heaney, whom, The Professor believed, was also overrated.

He chuckled again.

Then he realized the room had gone silent. He was still staring at the pretty student's impressive breasts. So he blinked and took off his glasses and cleaned them with his pocket handkerchief and cleared his throat and knew he had to say something. He normally didn't say much as students went around on the first day with their favorite writers, who were the writers they wanted to become, or who they wanted their peers to think they might become; even he could see that.

He felt he should say something to this poor girl, warn her off such misguided aspirations. He patted the book in front of him, the book he planned to read from at the end, the big finale. It was a hardcover, the dust jacket removed so no one could read the title or author's name. "She could have used a better editor," he said. "Just pages and pages of draff." He paused, tapped his book again, grinned suggestively. "But a wild drinker, wild life. I could tell you stories!"

The room was quiet. He cleared his throat.

He nodded at the next student, a broad-shouldered Asian-American man who awkwardly lifted the book he'd had his thumb pressed into this whole time, saving the page, waiting for his moment to read and talk about this particular page and these particular words. He looked first, very briefly, at the pretty girl. And then he began to speak in a voice that was too loud for the room.

The Professor could still tune him out. He thought again of the well-regarded writer he'd just maligned. He did not regret maligning her. But a glance at the pretty student's face and he could tell he'd hurt her. Her mouth was turned down, her eyes averted. For a moment he felt badly, but then he thought her hurt could turn out to be useful.

He was powerful. But not, when he examined it, in the way he wished to be powerful. He knew famous writers, and he knew rich people. He and his wife were, in fact, very rich and lived in a beautiful house and traveled frequently to Paris, where they had a second home. The combination of these facts gave him the kind of sheen of the near-famous, the power of proximity. He could get away with what he wanted to get away with because of the idea he might introduce people to either fame or fortune or both. He had done so once, many years ago—with a young writer who had received many awards—and so the suggestion remained (whispered in the halls) that he could and would do so again. He was just waiting for the right one. This girl might do.

He scanned the room. Eight men. Four women. It wasn't a great ratio for him. The boys looked energetic and hungry. They'd all get together after class to talk about workshop and to drink. He suspected they liked to throw back a few. The women—aside from the pretty one? One was too old, one very fat, and the last one, in the seat closest to him, but with one empty chair between them, was Black.

In her twenties, a beautiful age, but skinny as a blade of grass, no tits to speak of, with a thin, hard mouth.

When it finally came to her turn, he listened long enough to hear her say the name of her chosen writer, and the name at first delighted him—because he knew this man well—then irritated him immediately after.

For it was the name of the man he'd once been compared to most often: lauded New England novelist, master of prose, who The Professor knew for a fact—*everyone* knew—was a terrible womanizer, even though his third wife was incredibly beautiful, a former student, and totally unsuspecting. The Professor admired this writer, envied him, felt flashes of rage anytime he heard good literary news about the old man with the charmed life. He'd done some therapy about it, mostly unhelpful.

The Professor was rarely compared to the Charmed Writer anymore. In fact The Professor was *never* compared to him anymore or to any other writer, living or dead.

Without him realizing it, something had shifted in the room. This skinny girl had shifted it.

"I mean, yes," she was saying. "It's a gorgeous piece of writing. It's the story that made me want to become a writer." She paused, looked around the circle, eyes scornful the moment they glanced at The Professor, and continued, "But when I look at it now, I can see it's just bullshit. It's good writing—"masculine" writing, they like to say. But it's empty. All the women in this novel are just vessels for the men's sexual desires. They're not real."

There were some nods of agreement, even from the male students.

The Professor felt his irritation kick in again. "But that wasn't the assignment, was it?" he said.

Her gaze was piercing. "Pardon?"

"The assignment was to talk about a writer you admire, a writer whose work you love."

She smiled. Ever so slightly. When she smiled, he found her lovely.

"Well, I did admire him," she said. She spoke slowly now, confidently. And as she spoke, she radiated a glowing curiosity—which The Professor only recognized as beauty. "And now I don't anymore." She looked at him without blinking. "I thought that was an interesting way to consider the assignment: how what we love changes because what we understand changes."

The pretty girl agreed. "I love that idea. Who knows where we'll be when we graduate from here, what our writing will look like, who our favorite writers will be?"

One of the male students, a tall man with too much hair, said, "Plus, he's a total racist. Have you all read the story about the—"

Students were already nodding vehemently.

Now The Professor felt he had to come to the defense of the Charmed Writer, who he disliked, but whose name did not deserve this kind of attack. The man was a Pulitzer-prize winner!

"He's a really remarkable man, very progressive. His second wife was Chinese."

The girl who'd first attacked the Charmed Writer proceeded to—he couldn't believe this—to laugh.

"Good for him," she said, still laughing. And then she looked straight at him, and her smile faded. He felt her loveliness retreat. She did not look away. Suddenly he felt too hot, the pain in his lower back flared. He looked down at his shirt cuffs and rolled them up, taking his time. Something else radiated from her now, and he thought it best not to name it.

"Well!" he said. He had to bring things to a close. "I suppose it's my turn now."

And so he patted the book in front of him, the one he would read from. "I won't tell you the writer's name. Perhaps you will be able to guess."

The pretty student exchanged looks with the skinny one. He

didn't want to examine the look's meaning.

Initially, he had planned to read a passage from The Sound and the Fury, the book that had made him want to become a writer. But this afternoon while browsing the shelves of the neighborhood secondhand bookstore, he'd changed his mind.

And so he began to read the opening from his very own first novel, the best book he'd written, and honestly the favorite one he'd ever read:

"The end came unexpectedly for Edward. For everyone else, it came as no surprise."

The Professor paused. He looked around the table and knew, without a doubt, that his students were not listening to him.

He tried not to mind. He still found the words a beautiful surprise. He sometimes liked to read them out loud, sometimes to his wife, when she would let him. ("A triumphant first book," a critic had written. The same critic who later said about his third novel, "A dull little portrait of bourgeois domesticity.")

The Professor had heard the words of his first book as music when writing them and still wanted others to hear them in the same way. Yet he knew they did not. Because today he had found ten copies—four of them signed!—at the bookstore that he visited once a month with the express purpose of torturing himself.

This music was the opposite of torture. Reading his happy first book—a signed first edition he'd purchased today for $10!—was like falling in love for the first time. No, it was better than falling in love. As good as the first time he fucked an undergraduate student in his office, her huge tits in his hands, his mouth, her knees splayed on his velvet loveseat. (The second time she had cried and kept her clothes on and left right after.) He could remember the color of her hair (red), but he couldn't remember her name.

Oh, there was so much he did not remember! So much he did not know! For example, he did not know that wanting something desperately did not guarantee having it. He *suspected* as much, but he did not *know* it bodily, because for his entire life he had been given so much in exchange for doing very little, and this was a poor lesson for art.

Even after all these years of teaching, he did not know that wanting his students to revere him would only produce in them unintended effects: boredom, disrespect, and in the worst and most frequent case, hatred.

He *could* see that in the near future, and for the rest of the semester, he would approach the pretty student at campus literary events and tell her how pretty she looked, how flattering her blouse looked, and then make excuses to touch her: her arm, her hair, her pretty tits. These he would touch through a clever technique he had devised. All the girls wore scarves these days, and he would hook his fingers on either side and slowly adjust, so his hands would graze the contours of a girl's chest.

Alas, he could not see that everyone he tried this with understood what the trick was. And he could not see they warned each other about it. He could not see that though the pretty and polite student would not report him to the administration for his trick, the skinny student would, after watching him perform it on others.

He already suspected that his irritation with this student would soon turn to disgust. He *didn't* suspect that in just two months, another faculty member would confront him about the behavior she reported, the behavior everyone knew about already but only now felt they could talk about (because they had to or else: possible lawsuit). His response? He would tell his colleagues how terrible the skinny girl's writing was, even though it wasn't. Far from it! It terrified him how good her work was and how little he understood it.

He could not see that in spite of his treatment of her, that she would flourish. But not in his workshop, not in the program. That would prove a disappointment to her: alienating and sleepless. For years after graduating, she would barely write or talk to other writers. Instead, she would hop from job to job for a while: ESL instructor in Korea, copywriter in Seattle, textbook editor in Chicago. But eventually she would gather up the dreams of her former self, sit herself down every evening after work for twelve months straight, and she would write it all: all the terrible and beautiful things in her body and mind, and she would use them to conjure a story that would make her readers weep from joy and recognition and relief.

By then, The Professor would be long retired, and living a life many would envy: expensive and comfortable vacations, beautiful grandchildren, all the time he wanted to write. And oh, he would write. But he would not be happy. Especially the first time he opened the newspaper to see his former student's name on the Bestseller list. Though he would have forgotten her long ago, her name would ring a little warning bell. And he would be especially unhappy, though still unable to pinpoint why, when he saw the cover of her book in the window of his favorite bookstore in town (not the secondhand one). And when the program invited her to campus to give a reading, the current director would invite him in his capacity as Professor Emeritus, and he would attend, expecting a little pleasant fawning from current faculty and staff, but as soon as he saw his former student sitting in the front row, radiant and holding her glorious book, surrounded by young admirers now studying in the program, he would feel immediately ill and have to call his wife to bring the car around.

For now, though, he was delighted: reading his favorite novel aloud to an audience. He finished reading one page, and then he read another. He could recite the words from memory, but he enjoyed the way they looked on the page: a permanent record of his former mind. He suspected that the students who were pretending to take notes were merely writing their own future novels. But he did not care. He read until he couldn't anymore, until his eyes were too tired and his voice was thin and the sky outside the tall windows had gone completely dark.

The Man Running the Hiring Committee

You've got the search narrowed to two solid candidates—one man, Candidate A, and one woman, Candidate B. A is obviously the better fit. By all reasonable measures, he's accomplished more than most in his career: Ivy League education, glowing recommendations, paid speaking engagements, being white and straight.

But it isn't just the sheen of his accomplishments or his prior experience with six-figure salaries. You genuinely like him. And when you bring him in for an all-day interview, which includes dinner at the place with the cute waitresses, it turns out *everyone else likes him too!* He reminds Jack of his buddies from boarding school. He's just like David's frat brothers at Duke. Ambitious, of course. But he also knows how to have good time! Everyone agrees: He's the one.

Well, everyone except Jane, the woman on your hiring committee, who you had to include because, well, diversity. Not to knock Jane, who's pretty enough, but a bit of a downer.

"I don't think we should hire him," she says.

This is quintessential Jane. "Why not? He's perfect."

"I just got a bad vibe."

You try hard not to laugh. She sounds like your tween daughter.

"A bad *vibe*," Jack says. He and David exchange glances.

"He kept staring down my shirt when he thought I wasn't looking."

Now you and David exchange glances. There's not much to look at under her shirt, for crying out loud!

You don't plan to give Jane's whining a second thought. But later that night you tell your wife what Jane said, while you're crawling into bed. You think you're on your way to a quick, sleep-inducing roll in the hay after a mutually satisfying laugh at Jane's expense. But your wife gives you that look.

"What?"

"Listen to Jane."

"Jane's a killjoy. You said so yourself! You never want to invite her to our parties."

The look your wife continues to give you is one you've seen all your married life, but there's something new about it: She's not just annoyed; she's fucking pissed. And suddenly you realize she might actually leave you for her hot and sensitive yoga instructor, Raphael.

So the next day, imagining Raphael going down on your wife, you call up one of Candidate A's recommenders, his old boss, a guy who's been at it for a long time, who knows what's what.

"Oh, A!" he cries. "Everyone loves A. He gets great results."

You're about to say thanks and hang up, but you think of Jane. You think of Raphael bringing your wife breakfast in bed. You ask, "Was there ever any—"

"Any what?" There's a long, potent pause.

"Was he ever, you know. A creep? With women?"

The pause extends.

A's boss answers finally, slowly. "Well, there were, ah, rumors. Some women didn't feel . . . "

"Didn't feel what?"

"There were a couple of complaints to HR."

Later, you repeat this information to the hiring committee.

Jack frowns. "So?"

Jane frowns. "What do you mean, 'so'?"

David says, "You can't let a couple of rumors ruin a guy's life."

Right?! You give an internal fist bump to Jack and David. Your wife's not going to leave you for fucking Raphael! He's got terrible BO, and your wife is very sensitive to smells.

"Innocent until proven guilty, right?"

Jack and David nod. Jane does not nod.

She says, "This is a goddamn job interview, not a criminal investigation. Candidate B has no rumors about misconduct following her. And she's got basically the same resume."

"But she's not a good fit," Jack says.

"She really isn't," David says.

"Not the best," you agree. She had *a lot* of ideas, and she wasn't above inserting them into the conversation.

In the end, you're willing to make the call: Candidate A all the way. Even if it means losing your wife. Because that's the kind of sacrifice you have to make sometimes. To do what's right for your fellow man.

Everyone Gets It

Did you ever happen to think . . . reality's being changed out from under us, replaced, renewed, all the time—only we don't know it?

—Ursula K. Le Guin, *The Lathe of Heaven*

Cici in Social Media has returned from vacation with a new personal belief system. "In the end," she informs me, "everyone gets what they want."

It's 9:05 AM, eleven days before the election, and I haven't heard her voice for almost a week, so I'm barely invested in the emails in my inbox, let alone Cici's latest revelation. Her hair looks almost soaking wet, but she tells me that's just this new hair spray she scored at duty free.

"What do you mean, *everyone* gets what they want?"

"Just what it sounds like! People get their deepest wishes, whether they realize it or not."

"You mean like that thing on *Oprah*—what was it—*The Secret*?"

Cici's ideas about work and life are often derivative of something that's already been done in popular culture, but she'll never admit it.

"I don't think I've heard of that one," she says.

Her blouse is peach silk and sheer under the fluorescent lights. I can see the embroidery on her camisole: tiny, thorny roses. Her travel mug is from the Starbucks at the Charles de Gaulle Airport, and as she leans over my cubicle wall, she makes sure the Eiffel Tower is facing toward me.

Even so, I don't ask about her trip to Paris.

It doesn't matter. She launches into one of her stories. The kind that begin with her home in bed on a Friday night after fucking a guy and really enjoying it physically but emotionally still feeling like something is missing.

In the middle of the night, the disappointing guy in question snoring in her bed, she bought a ticket to Paris for the following day. Not because she'd always dreamed of going, but because a friend on Instagram posted a picture of herself in front of the Mona Lisa at the Louvre, and Cici has always loved that painting because it reminds her that she doesn't have to smile to be respected.

"So you went to Paris because you don't want to have to smile?"

"The point I'm trying to make is . . . "

She finally just cashed in her stored up vacation days, flew economy class but drank herself to sleep on the plane so she didn't even mind not having leg room, landed in Paris, and asked the cab driver to take her straight to the Eiffel Tower. Once she was at the top and buffeted by tender winds and gazing out at this spectacular view of the most romantic city on earth, she realized she had finally done *exactly what she wanted*: struck out on her own without a plan, and discovered she was happy alone.

Since she's been talking, my inbox has begun filling up. I see my digital calendar is now pink with meetings the project managers have inserted into my day. A deep sadness behind my eyes catches me by surprise; I try to tease out its origin. Minutes ago I was happy—happy enough—and I look straight into Cici's eyes—heavily mascaraed with what I know from prior exchanges is a brand for which she is willing to drive five hours to a department store in Chicago.

"Did you get to the Louvre?"

She smiles. "I met someone."

"I thought—"

"At the top of the Eiffel Tower! Romantic, right?"

"Weren't you alone there, discovering yourself?"

My sudden sadness has merged with extreme irritation and become this lumpen thing in my chest. I click off my desk lamp and gather my things for the 9:30 conference call with the brand managers from Gorgeous Hair. Chip, their head, is a real ass; I have to brace myself because he likes to tear down all my ideas for taglines right before telling me what to say, which is always what I just said with an additional word. (It takes everything I've got not to ask what a bald guy knows about volumizing shampoo.)

Cici walks with me solemnly, as if to a court appointment, and puts her hand on my shoulder just outside the green room—so called because it once had a green carpet that our best graphic designer, Anh, tore out in anger last year while working on a project for Audi through the weekend. Those guys were the biggest assholes. Anh is funny and amazing and hates the same people I do. The green room is now a deep purple that gives me a headache.

Just as I open the door, I hear someone inside say, "I'd rather vote for Trump than have to listen to Chip this morning."

Cici whispers, "You'll get what you want too, Emma."

9:30 to noon: Chip spends the Gorgeous meeting complaining on a bad phone line about how bad the phone line is, and then he complains about "the look" of our most recent campaign, which he says wasn't innovative enough; the Creative Team follows this meeting up with another meeting complaining about Chip's complaints. And then comes lunchtime in the break room, which is unbearable. The twenty-four-year-old engineers play foosball and drink Gatorade and shout-talk about bands coming through town, bands whose names make me feel very old. (Better Sex, Weed Killers, Plague Upon Your Ass.)

A table of account managers eat their small salads and sip their giant iced lattes. They wave me over. They're all very nice individually, but I get anxious when they're in a group. They used to publicly discuss my future here, which they said looked bright. "You're a natural storyteller," Fiona with the smooth hair used to say. Now she just tries to put me on all her accounts because she knows I'll do the work quickly, without complaining.

"Emma, you never eat with us!" she says now.

I point to the fridge and shrug. I'm just there to microwave my leftovers.

But I'm in such a rush to get away that my leftovers are still cold when I get back to my cubicle, and I eat them while scrolling through the mommy blog of a girl I went to school with, the first girl I kissed. We both loved reading The Baby-Sitters Club Books and would pass them around as if they were contraband. In high school she started trying to turn me on to Jesus, and I went to Sunday school with her once, just so I could squeeze next to her in the hard pew and smell her almond shampoo. But it felt like the walls were literally closing in on me when the pastor told me the Lord loved me and was happy to see a fresh face in church. Then my friend went on to a teensy Christian college on full scholarship, I went to an elite private one that I went into debt for. From her blog I've learned she lives in our slightly rundown hometown in a mansion with her snowmobile-dealer husband.

I rarely go back to my hometown anymore. It's too exhausting. But where isn't exhausting? The town I've ended up alone in is a little glossy for my taste. It feels like an advertisement for the kind of place you'd like to live in. If the kind of place you liked to live in were filled primarily with opportunities to buy locally made cheese and "art" made of rusted metal.

My ex turned out to be that kind of person. She filled one wall of our living room with decorative oak leaves cast in copper. I left her, but for some reason haven't been able to leave the town.

1:00 to 4:30: pointless meeting, ten minutes of writing copy for an app that will buy your groceries for you, fifteen minutes of listening to Cici tell Anh about her plans for the weekend (live her life to the fullest or something).

At 4:45, Anh's beautiful head peers over her cubicle at me, a look of desperation in her eyes. I can see she needs an intervention because at this rate, she will die before we get to elect the first woman President.

But then comes 4:50 PM and Jeff, our "creative director," appears between me and Anh. He hovers a foot from my cubicle, wearing his usual gray hoodie. This one says Source Code, a band I'm pretty sure he only pretends to love so the hipster engineers will let him talk to them.

He always looks relieved to have a half-wall between us. He's got his Diet Coke in one hand, his phone in the other, a guy who always needs a prop.

"So, Emma . . . " he begins, and I know right away he's about to give me a last-minute project, which means an account executive probably gave him some work to do four hours ago, but he's been playing video games with Ronnie, a project manager who irons his khakis (I know because I overheard Cici tell Anh. Cici used to date Ronnie, and so obviously I know a lot about Ronnie.)

"I was hoping to get home in time to watch *Dr. Phil*," I say.

"You like *Dr. Phil?*" Jeff says, smiling a little. "I *luuuv*—"

"Of course I don't like Dr. Phil, Jeffrey. He manipulates people's emotional traumas for ratings."

"Oh, okay. Sure. Guilty pleasure, I guess—"

"What do you want me to do at this very late hour, Jeffrey?"

Embarrassed, flustered, and relieved, he explains: he needs me to edit an important deck, a PowerPoint presentation for the president. Big meeting tomorrow between heads of Creative and Account and Management. There's a potential new client, an important client. His small gray eyes are glittery with nerves. We all know the agency's on thin ice right now since we lost a couple of big accounts in the spring.

"Everything's in the deck already," he says. "I just want to make sure there aren't any typos."

"Send me the creative brief with the file."

He goes away quickly, raising his Diet Coke in a gesture of thanks.

As soon as he emails me the PowerPoint, I groan so loudly that Cici and Anh come over and look at the file open on my monitor.

"Jesus," Anh says. "What a dick."

Half the slides are empty except for a few bullet points. "Guess I'm gonna miss *Dr. Phil*."

"I'll stay and help," Anh says.

"I'd stay too," Cici says, "but I have a FaceTime date with my French lover." She giggles while putting on her camel-colored coat, which she also bought in Paris.

"Serenity!" she says, on her way out the door. "I have good feeling about this account, ladies."

Serenity is a line of very expensive yoga pants. Everyone knows Cici loves Serenity because she always posts selfies of her doing yoga in them.

While Cici daydreams about free yoga pants, Anh and I get some work done. I browse Serenity's website for their basic look and feel (graceful serif fonts, neutral colors that wouldn't offend anyone) as well as their key messaging—*breathe beautifully*. Anh puts together three designs to use in various parts of the presentation. They're artful, simple images—silhouettes of women doing yoga on backgrounds that could be anywhere—the beach, the desert—and even though I don't do yoga, I suddenly want to slip into something more comfortable.

"I'm pretty sure Jeff knew this would happen," Anh says. "That we'd be working on this together."

"If he'd only asked us four hours ago, we could have been home by now."

But I'm not really complaining. It's not bad in the office when it's quiet. The lights on the creative side have dimmed. Only our two desk lights are on.

I'm sure Anh can tell I'm a little in love with her. It doesn't matter. She has a boyfriend who is dreamy in an annoying way and brings her flowers on random days, just because.

Anh is chuckling to herself, and then I see an incoming email from her, and I open it: She has photoshopped Jeff's head under the foot of a woman in Warrior One.

I laugh so hard I start to cry. Anh laughs too, and the bright sound fills the entire office.

Once we stop laughing, we finish polishing up the presentation, I email it to Jeff, and Anh and I turn off our computers.

In the parking lot, there is a new chill in the air. Our breaths come out in little clouds.

"Thanks, Anh, you're the best."

She smiles. "Someone needs to be around here."

She gets in her little blue Honda, I get in my shitty diesel VW that I'll be reimbursed for eventually, but who the hell knows when.

In spite of what I know to be true, I hear Cici's words from the morning on a loop on my drive home. I find myself asking: do people really get what they want? As if this is actually a puzzle to work out.

Did Jeff get what he wanted? He wore a fucking hoodie to his interview here four months ago. And even though the two women the president brought in before him were dressed in classy suits on top of being poised and qualified and in possession of some humor, they were deemed less "leaderly" by the hiring committee.

The hiring committee apparently went crazy for Jeff's personal tagline: *Born digital*. It's on all his business cards.

The truth is he grew up with the same kind of phone I did, the one with a rotary dial, and played *The Oregon Trail* on a floppy disk in computer classes in elementary school.

He's forty, just a few years older than me and one year younger than Anh, who should really have his job but hates management and didn't even bother applying for it, even though the whole creative team begged her to because everyone loves Anh.

My secret from Anh and the creative team is that I threw my hat in the ring too. Why not? People like me enough because I don't gossip—not because I don't judge everyone but because I prefer to judge silently, without the interference of human conversation.

The important thing though is that our clients generally like my ideas. Even if they don't know the ideas are mine.

I am keeping my secret though because I didn't even get an interview. It was weird watching the tiny parade of women they brought in, and weirder still to be disappointed when they didn't get the job I wanted.

Did I really want the job though? Given Cici's logic, one would have to say no. But given my bank account, one would think I might be interested in someday paying off my college loans.

In the morning, there is a mouse in the trap on the kitchen counter. My ex would have taken care of it, but now I have to. I turn on NPR. The news is gloomy. New Clinton emails, supposedly. It'll be nothing, it always is, but I still hear the headline like a weight in my stomach. I put on dishwashing gloves and squint my eyes so the dead mouse body is just a gray blur, and then I lift up the trap, throw it in the trash, and have a good cry.

Friday morning I'm late, so by the time I arrive at work there's only one space left in the lot, the one that's right next to the lamppost I often crash my door into. On the other side is a beige Bronco I don't recognize, and it's over the line, which makes me even more irritated. I peek inside and in the back seat, just sort of innocently lying there is a red ball cap, and my chest tightens, but the little white letters just spell L-O-V-E.

Things don't improve when Cici comes by my desk first thing, begging me to write some copy for a quiz Gorgeous Hair is running on their Facebook page. "You always have the best headlines," she says.

"Not today, Cici."

"Did you hear the latest about the Clinton emails?" she says, voice trembling.

I nod but keep walking to the break room.

The last thing I want to do is talk politics before more coffee. During the midterm elections in 2010, I made the mistake of telling Cici, who grew up here, that I hadn't voted, and it was the only time she ever spoke sternly to me. "Where's your sense of civic responsibility?" she scolded before launching into a lecture about how her first time voting was a midterm election, and her guy won his election for local county legislator. "It felt so good it was practically orgasmic!" Cici said. "Of course, just a year into his term he was embroiled in a corruption scandal and then punched a reporter in the face. He had to resign. But oh, what a thrill it was to win!"

At noon Jeff calls us into the green room for an important brainstorming session. He's so smiley he looks like a baby version of Jeff—a little dimply and mischievous—and this almost makes him sympathetic. But then he claims that it was his beautiful deck that persuaded management to give our team the go ahead to start brainstorming a pitch for Serenity. I'm used to Jeff taking credit for work that isn't his own, but right now it's hard not to walk out.

The next thing that comes out of Jeff's mouth is familiar too: he's looking for "big ideas."

What's new? I scribble on a notepad and shove in front of Anh.

She scribbles back, *New hoodie.* I look at Jeff again and see that, indeed, his scarlet hoodie is a new one in the rotation. His usual hue is gray. I can't help it, the sudden color shift makes me suspicious, and I scribble back, *Think he's a—*

But before I can finish, Jeff clears his throat. He's looking at me in that scared-mad way new teachers look at their difficult students.

"Thoughts, Emma?" He points a soft, thick finger to the question he's just written on the board: *What do women want (from yoga pants)?*

Ronnie raises his hand. There's a coffee stain the shape of a carnation blooming around the button above his belt. "I might have a good one," he says, then looks around the table, landing on Cici, then Anh, then me, the only actual women in the room, and joke-winces. "Don't want to get shot down though . . . "

Jeff says, "It's always good to get an outsider's perspective." He gives me a don't-make-this-hard look. "Go ahead, Ronnie."

"I want to say that women want to look beautiful—that they do yoga to look beautiful for their husbands."

"Excellent start, Ronnie. Excellent." He writes that down.

"What if a woman doesn't have, or even want a husband?" Anh says.

"Sure, sure," Jeff says, "but, and this is a good reminder for all of us: no idea is wrong." He beams. "And of course some women *do* want to look beautiful for their husbands and boyfriends."

Anh rolls her eyes behind Jeff's back, then slips the paper from under my fingertips and scribbles something else. *When are we running away together to Toronto?*

For a second, I see us crossing the border hand in hand, and although I've always found Canada kind of boring, I am filled with sudden enthusiasm.

But then Pete, another copywriter who's decent at his job and usually keeps his inane remarks to himself, says something about how yoga pants are stretchy—"Good for breakup binge-eating," he says.

Jeff grins and writes that down, pressing the tip of the dry erase marker hard on the board.

Pete at least has the good sense to blush when I glare at him.

I feel Cici taking in a breath, the way she does before she's about to deliver one of her monologues.

"What I'm wondering," she says, "is if we shouldn't be opening up the question a little more."

Jeff frowns at the whiteboard. Cici can't see him.

"Why aren't we asking," she continues, "what *people* want?"

The room is silent for a full three seconds.

Then Cici talks for the rest of the meeting. At first it's mostly drivel and some of it is about a potential launch on Facebook involving photos women and men and children—there is a kids' line, Child's Pose—would take wearing their Serenity pants, in their favorite places, doing their favorite yoga positions. (Ronnie laughs at the word "positions.")

In truth, Cici probably spends fifteen full minutes reminiscing about Autumn Moonbeam, a yoga teacher who inspired Cici to get her life together.

Autumn Moonbeam (not her original name) had spent time in state prison for cocaine possession and distribution her first year of college. In jail, surrounded by despair, she started to exercise. She started to practice the yoga her society-loving Manhattan mother had practiced her whole life. Soon, she found other women joining her in her morning sun salutations. The despair started to lift for Autumn. She was out on parole in less than a year because her counselor saw her growth. She went on to be a world-renowned yoga teacher and now has a whole line of successful meditation videos.

Cici pauses.

Jeff says, "I don't really think prison is the message Serenity wants to send out?"

Cici smiles patiently. "Listen to the story, Jeff: *Yoga sets you free.*"

"Yoga sets white girls free, maybe?" I say.

Instead of looking at me, everyone's eyes dart nervously to Anh and away, which happens every time anyone brings up race.

Anh rolls her eyes. Cici gazes at Jeff, her expression triumphant. She whisper-shouts: "Yoga sets *everybody* free."

After the meeting, Jeff comes to my desk and asks me to walk with him to his office. He spends ten minutes talking about his grievances against the latest iPhone, while he scrolls through photos of his family's recent vacation in Cancún. He stops complaining long enough to say how much his kids loved ordering virgin piña coladas at the resort's swim-up bar.

I've started to zone out when I hear him say my name. "Emma? Are you with me?"

"Sorry?"

"We can't let Cici take over this account." His voice has gone hoarse and a little ugly, but he has my attention now.

"Actually, I thought her Facebook idea was okay."

"Cici doesn't get to choose the direction here."

"Okay—"

"This means I need to see some leadership from you on Serenity. This is a big account. We need to win it."

"Of course, Boss," I say. "I'll lead my yoga-toned ass off."

"That's just what we need: someone with real no-nonsense yoga experience."

"Do I look like I actually do yoga, Jeffrey?"

"Um—" He looks down for a second, then back at me. "Okay! Good! Pitch meeting's on Monday afternoon in Cincinnati. That means we need a campaign direction end of day today."

His grin starts out nervous but gradually snakes up his face until it hits his eyes. "You don't have any plans to watch *Dr. Phil* tonight, do ya?" He laughs, a hard little bark.

"No, but I did have plans to lie in bed dreaming of stabbing you through your iPhone-holding hand."

Of course I don't say that.

I do leave the room smiling, with a corner of hatred for Jeff in my heart.

Anh, Ronnie, Pete, and I are asked to stay late to nail down a creative direction on Serenity. We're in the blue room this time—blue for walls the color of ink, not much better than the green room to be honest, but the table's bigger here and we can spread out all our papers, our laptops, our notepads and sketches of yoga pants doing tree pose without a body in them.

All around us are cans of Diet Coke and wrappers from subs we had delivered, but Ronnie's still hungry at 8:00 PM when we're stalled on a real direction for a potential campaign.

I know it's going to be a long night when Ronnie starts arguing outside the Blue Room with the pizza delivery guy over whether Hillary Clinton should be put in federal or state prison. Ronnie says state; he doesn't want her to get any of the cushy benefits of his federal tax dollars. Pizza guy says let her have her sheets with the nice thread count, the better to hang herself with, and even when Ronnie hands over the tip they continue imagining a nice jail house cell for HRC.

I've been writing terrible yoga-related taglines all evening, and now I make another one on my notepad and show it to Anh and Pete:

Yoga for All

White Women Do Yoga

Serenity Now

I'm Losing It, People

Pete shrugs and shares his own taglines:

Do these Yoga Pants Make My Ass Look Hot?

Putting the Hot in Hot Yoga

Not Your Mother's Yoga Pants

Pete says, "They're shit. Sorry."

But now I have an idea. "They're exactly what Jeff wants."

This is how we end up, by 1:00 AM, building an entire, imaginary ad campaign around hot chicks with their hot mothers doing yoga together in their Serenity pants, which they receive at a discount when they submit an Instagram photo of them doing handstands in their favorite, picturesque place.

Sure, that last idea is pretty much Cici's, but Jeff won't even notice with all the other shit we've put around it, and in the end he'll like the idea so much he'll be sure it was his.

Between Friday night and Saturday morning, a thunderstorm kicks up outside, and I come down with the worst case of the flu I've had since every Christmas of my childhood. I mean throwing up until there's no more left to throw up. I can't leave the bathroom.

I get a text from Anh: *You okay? I think I got food poisoning.*

I text back: *The fucking pizza.*

Anh writes up a complaint on Yelp and emails the link to me. After throwing up once more for good measure, I add in my two cents, which includes a suggestion that the delivery guy keep both his E. coli and misogyny to himself next time.

Monday morning, I haul myself out of bed, drive to work, and on the way see tree limbs scattered about the damp road. Our office is in a mini-industrial park at the edge of town on what used to be swampland. It still floods here sometimes, so I'm not surprised to see the pools of water in the parking lot. I'm on the early side today so the lot is empty, but when I go inside, the quiet and dark are unnerving.

Our secretary, Debra, says there's been a power outage and none of our computers are working. I've never seen her look happier.

I'm sitting at my desk in front of my dark computer, when I hear a little whisper, "Kind of spooky in here, isn't it?"

I jump a little. It's Cici, giant latte in hand, still wearing her coat.

"Jesus, you look terrible," she says. "You should go home and stay in bed. President says the power won't be back on till end of day."

"What about the pitch meeting?"

Cici narrows her eyes. "For Serenity? You guys went ahead on that without me?"

"We—"

"You don't have to explain, Emma." She keeps walking. "I know who to blame."

While lying on the couch at home with my laptop on my stomach, I get an email from Jeff about how much he loves our work: *You nailed it, kiddo. Now I know why you were almost considered for my job. Guess I better watch my back, huh?* ☺

I throw up again, luckily not on my laptop keyboard, but I still make a mess on the floor.

Pitch meeting with Serenity gets moved to Monday of the following week. I call in sick until then. At first it's not the best decision. I just end up lying on the couch all of Tuesday, listening to nonstop election coverage.

Anh texts me: *You okay?*

Me: *No*

Anh: *Turn off the radio. Get off the internet.*

So I do.

For about fifteen minutes.

I fall asleep while reading the latest *New York Times* poll, which still puts Hillary ahead by twenty percentage points. It doesn't make me feel any better. My dreams are newsreels of recent head-lines, narrated by the voice of my ex, who was born in London. Her accent was the primary reason I loved her at first; she could convince me of anything.

I only wake when I hear knocking at the door. I rise slowly. By the time I get to the door there's no one there, but someone has left a paper bag from one of the many places in town where you can buy local cheese—and all other sorts of expensive things in fancy packaging. Inside the bag is an artisanal ginger beer and some stone-ground wheat crackers made at a nice bakery in town. There's a card too, and as I open it my heart flutters a little, thinking of Anh dropping off this rescue meal for me.

But it's not from Anh. The card says:

Feel better soon. The office needs you.

Cici

I finally feel human by Monday. I drive to the office early so that we can carpool to Cincinnati together for the pitch, but when I arrive, Anh's at her desk, not smiling.

"Jeff decided at the last minute they didn't need us. He wanted to take the lead on the pitch."

I picture Jeff doing his best Don Draper impression with our misguided campaign strategy. I'm pretty sure Serenity's going to hate the work. A small space opens up in my chest, but the joy doesn't rush in like I thought it would. "And the president went for it?"

Anh laughs without mirth. "Our fearless leader? That guy's judgment is the whole reason we're in the hole in the first place. Audi? American Coffee? We lost those accounts because he puts the most incompetent people on the biggest campaigns."

"So the agency is doomed, pretty much."

"We're all doomed, Emma."

On Tuesday morning I vote anyway. And find myself crying from a momentary hope and pride in my little voting booth in the church up the street from my house.

On Instagram I see a selfie of Cici in a pantsuit and an "I Voted" sticker with the caption *Fierce Feminist*. And although selfies are not generally in my wheelhouse, I take one outside in the parking lot and give it a caption: *Just voted for the first woman President*. After posting it, a shiver runs through my whole body.

In the office, people are smiling and wearing their own stickers and drinking their locally roasted coffees.

Then 1:00 PM rolls around and there's a subtle shift in the atmosphere. I swear I hear a scream from the back of the office.

The news starts trickling in:

Serenity is going with Invention, a bigger agency in Chicago.

Serenity hated our pitch. Mostly though, they hated Jeff; he wore a hoodie to the meeting and the Serenity CEO, a woman in her late twenties, was not impressed.

By the end of the day, there is more news:

Jeff has been fired.

Someone reports seeing him just sitting at his desk, grasping his can of Diet Coke.

I'm starting to feel a little better, but then Cici comes by my desk, pulls up a chair, and tells me Anh has resigned and accepted an offer from Invention.

I start pushing my chair back. I have to find Anh and tell her not to go, that she needs to stay and steer this sinking ship.

But Cici puts her hand on my arm. She's still talking in a loud whisper, this time about Jeff: the two of them had been sleeping together for months until she flew to Paris, effectively breaking it off forever. Ever since he's been sending her angry texts and emails, which she forwarded to the president last night.

She leans in and says, very close to my ear, "I think you'll be getting an offer soon."

She grins, but before I can respond, she has left the building.

The next day, a pall has descended on the office. No one speaks. In the break room Fiona is sobbing into a young engineer's arms. Cici calls in sick. Ronnie emails me a few assignments and signs all of his messages *#MAGA, Make Advertising Great Again.*

I wait all day for an email from the president, or a call into his office with an offer of a new title. Nothing comes.

The next morning it's dark in the office, and I'm at my desk eating breakfast and reading my old pal's blog. You'd never know there'd just been a Presidential election. Her latest post is about the snow-mobile market. With the decline in snowfall in our hometown and all around the north of the state, snowmobile sales have been down in the last two years, and it's becoming a real financial concern. There's no mention of climate change—my old friend doesn't be-lieve in it—but I almost feel a little sorry that her family can't go to Disney in the New Year.

I hear someone saying my name behind me. It's Anh beckon-ing from her cubicle, and my body stiffens, knowing she'll be gone soon.

But when she smiles I feel light again. Her hair shimmers, and her arms are so taut from rock climbing; even on a cool fall day she's wearing a sleeveless top to show them off. I walk right to her, leaving my sad little yogurt cup beside my keyboard.

"Let's get out of here," she says, and I don't ask where to. We just go.

Acknowledgments

My gratitude to the editors of the following publications, where a number of these stories initially appeared: *Hobart* ("Affective Memory"); *Michigan Quarterly Review* ("The Invention of Love"); *Day One* and *Storyfront* ("House Hunting"); *Burrow Press Review* ("We Are Ready"); *The Missouri Review BLAST* ("West Lake"); *Inkwell* and *Redux* ("Our Lady of Guazá"); *Kenyon Review Online* ("My Husband's Second Wife"); *Bodega* ("The All Clear"); *Anomaly* ("Claire Tells a Story"); *CutBank Online* ("The Man Running the Hiring Committee"); *Joyland* ("Everyone Gets It").

I'm especially thankful to those editors whose insights made these stories better: Carmen Johnson, Ben Gwin, and Melissa Swantkowski. Thanks always to Greg Schutz for being the best reader and friend a writer could hope for.

I'm grateful to the amazing Kristine Langley Mahler for falling for this book and bringing it into the Split Lip Press family. Thanks to Caleb Tankersley for graceful editing and to Jayme Cawthern for the gorgeous design. My dear friend Thuy-Van Vu's painting is on the cover, which makes me so happy; I've loved her and her art from day one.

I wrote these stories during periods of uncertainty and distress— while unemployed, while barely sleeping with a newborn, while on the job market and moving from one state to another (and then another), and during and after the 2016 election. But I also wrote during periods of great joy, and the writing itself made me happy and grateful. Thanks to Natalia Singer for her friendship, which has gotten me through days of uncertainty. Thanks to all my daughter's teachers and daycare providers for providing structure to her days and mine, and for bringing our family joy by loving and teaching so well. Thanks especially to Janet Gregory and Saless Maxwell at the wonderful Oberlin Early Childhood Center.

My forever thanks to Ben and Iris. You make the gray days bright.

About the Author

Sara Schaff is the author of the story collection *Say Something Nice About Me* (Augury Books), and her writing has appeared in *Kenyon Review Online, The Yale Review Online, Literary Hub, Michigan Quarterly Review*, and elsewhere. An assistant professor of English at the State University of New York at Plattsburgh, she has taught at the University of Michigan, Oberlin College, and St. Lawrence University, as well as in China, Colombia, and Northern Ireland. Sara lives with her husband and daughter in Northern New York.

Now Available From

Split/Lip Press

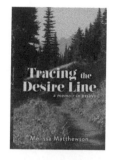

For more info about the press and our titles, visit

www.splitlippress.com

Follow us on Twitter and Instagram: @splitlippress

CPSIA information can be obtained
at www.ICGtesting.com
Printed in the USA
LVHW040125301221
707431LV00005B/581